NORTH POINT PRESS *San Francisco* *1988*

Open Door

STORIES BY

Luisa

Valenzuela

Translated by
Hortense Carpentier
J. Jorge Castello
Helen Lane
Christopher Leland
Margaret Sayers Peden
David Unger

Stories in the second and third part of
this book have been selected by the
author from the collections *Clara* and
Strange Things Happen Here,
originally published by Harcourt,
Brace, Jovanovich, New York. "The
Censors" appeared in *Short Shorts*,
edited by Irving Howe and Ilana Howe
and published by David Godine,
Boston.
English translations by Hortense
Carpentier and J. Jorge Castello are
reprinted from *Clara* by Luisa
Valenzuela, by permission of Harcourt,
Brace, Jovanovich. English translation
copyright © 1976 by Harcourt, Brace,
Jovanovich.
English translations by Helen Lane are
reprinted from *Strange Things Happen
Here* by Luisa Valenzuela by
permission of Harcourt, Brace,
Jovanovich. English translation
copyright © 1979 by Harcourt, Brace,
Jovanovich.

Contents

· *Open Door*

Preface

At seventeen I wrote my first real short story, "City of the Un-known," slipping into my mother's footsteps. She was a writer, and I didn't realize then that it was my first transgression: moving from passive devotion of her writing to desacralized emulation.

You don't steal what you inherit, as the saying in Spanish goes. Hermes stole and poetry was much better off for that, but one does what one can and it is exhilarating to discover that there are fresh and new and personal monsters behind every door one tries to force open.

For those discoveries and so much more I want to dedicate this freshly minted collection to the memory of Luisa Mercedes Levinson, my mother, and to the memory of her joy with literature, the way she and Borges used to laugh while writing a short story in collaboration, the memory of all those wonderful writers who were so often visiting, in particular to

Conrado Nalé Roxlo and his alter ego, Chamico—humor being the most precious tool of this extended family.

All this is not meant to explain why I chose the title *Open Door* when the idea of this selection was presented to me. Though I must confess that *Open Door* is the name of the most traditional, least threatening lunatic asylum in Argentina.

Are we all, in a way, inmates of the short story? As in our classic madhouse in the middle of the pampas, we can walk in and out of the short story whenever we please, but. And it is in this *but*, in this suspension between two beliefs or two doubts (one and the same thing) where the story is alive in us and we are alive in the story.

I would like to follow the hiatus or thread intertwining my stories through these three decades. The thread diverts, forks, becomes a spiderweb, and I am caught in a trap of my own devising.

My first collection, *Los Heréticos*, was published in 1967. Most of the stories were written while living in France, for three years, becoming a fascinated peeping tom to the magic in Brittany. Nothing was more tempting for me, then (and now!) than to walk in writing the tightrope between religious fanaticism and heresy. Of course heresy has the strongest pull.

I dislike dogmas and certainties. I delve in ambiguity, in that reflective field where reality appears at its most real. (So "Legend of the Selfsufficient Child" was caught in its own trap, becoming even ambiguous in its location in the different collections.)

For many years a couple of novels, changing loves, travels, and so forth distracted me from the short story. I went back to it in 1975, upon returning to my city after a long absence to find it wasn't mine any longer. Buenos Aires belonged then to violence and to state terrorism, and I could only sit in cafés and brood. Till I decided a book of short stories could be written in a month, at those same café tables, overhearing scraps of

· *Open Door*

scared conversations, seeping in the general paranoia. *Strange Things Happen Here* was born, and with it a new political awareness. And action. Which lead to other stories that have yet to appear, and this book.

On the other hand "Up Among the Eagles" (1983) took long years till it was somewhat completed. There is so much more I want to say about my love for Latin America and my passion for reinventing its myths.

For the time being, here are my favorite stories from the three collections. But I must hurry, now, and write others: it is the only way I know of jamming a foot in the door so it won't slam on our faces.

Open Door

Up

Among

the

Eagles

to Susan Sontag
and Ambrosio Vecino

The Censors

Poor Juan! One day they caught him with his guard down before he could even realize that what he had taken as a stroke of luck was really one of fate's dirty tricks. These things happen the minute you're careless, as one often is. Juancito let happiness—a feeling you can't trust—get the better of him when he received from a confidential source Mariana's new address in Paris and knew that she hadn't forgotten him. Without thinking twice, he sat down at his table and wrote her a letter. *The* letter that now keeps his mind off his job during the day and won't let him sleep at night (what had he scrawled, what had he put on that sheet of paper he sent to Mariana?).

Juan knows there won't be a problem with the letter's contents, that it's irreproachable, harmless. But what about the rest? He knows that they examine, sniff, feel, and read between the lines of each and every letter, and check its tiniest comma and most accidental stain. He knows that all letters pass from hand to hand and go through all sorts of tests in the huge censorship offices and that, in the end, very few continue on their way. Usually it takes months, even years, if there aren't any snags; all this time the freedom, maybe even the life, of both sender and receiver is in jeopardy. And that's why Juan's so troubled: thinking that something might happen to Mariana because of his letters. Of all people, Mariana, who must finally feel safe there where she always dreamt she'd live. But he knows that the *Censor's Secret Command* operates all over the world and cashes in on the discount in air fares; there's nothing to stop them from going as far as that hidden Paris neighborhood, kidnapping Mariana, and returning to their cozy homes, certain of having fulfilled their noble mission.

Well, you've got to beat them to the punch, do what everyone tries to do: sabotage the machinery, throw sand in its gears, get to the bottom of the problem so as to stop it.

This was Juan's sound plan when he, like many others, applied for a censor's job—not because he had a calling or needed a job: no, he applied simply to intercept his own letter, a consoling albeit unoriginal idea. He was hired immediately, for each day more and more censors are needed and no one would bother to check on his references.

Ulterior motives couldn't be overlooked by the *Censorship Division*, but they needn't be too strict with those who applied. They knew how hard it would be for the poor guys to find the letter they wanted and even if they did, what's a letter or two when the new censor would snap up so many others? That's how Juan managed to join the *Post Office's Censorship Division*, with a certain goal in mind.

The building had a festive air on the outside that contrasted with its inner staidness. Little by little, Juan was absorbed by his job, and he felt at peace since he was doing everything he could to get his letter for Mariana. He didn't even worry when, in his first month, he was sent to *Section K* where envelopes are very carefully screened for explosives.

· *Open Door*

It's true that on the third day, a fellow worker had his right hand blown off by a letter, but the division chief claimed it was sheer negligence on the victim's part. Juan and the other employees were allowed to go back to their work, though feeling less secure. After work, one of them tried to organize a strike to demand higher wages for unhealthy work, but Juan didn't join in; after thinking it over, he reported the man to his superiors and thus got promoted.

You don't form a habit by doing something once, he told himself as he left his boss's office. And when he was transferred to *Section J*, where letters are carefully checked for poison dust, he felt he had climbed a rung in the ladder.

By working hard, he quickly reached *Section E* where the job became more interesting, for he could now read and analyze the letters' contents. Here he could even hope to get hold of his letter, which, judging by the time that had elapsed, had gone through the other sections and was probably floating around in this one.

Soon his work became so absorbing that his noble mission blurred in his mind. Day after day he crossed out whole paragraphs in red ink, pitilessly chucking many letters into the censored basket. These were horrible days when he was shocked by the subtle and conniving ways employed by people to pass on subversive messages; his instincts were so sharp that he found behind a simple "the weather's unsettled" or "prices continue to soar" the wavering hand of someone secretly scheming to overthrow the Government.

His zeal brought him swift promotion. We don't know if this made him happy. Very few letters reached him in *Section B*—only a handful passed the other hurdles—so he read them over and over again, passed them under a magnifying glass, searched for microprint with an electronic microscope, and tuned his sense of smell so that he was beat by the time he made it home. He'd barely manage to warm up his soup, eat some fruit, and fall into bed, satisfied with having done his duty. Only his darling mother worried, but she couldn't get him back on the right track. She'd say, though it wasn't always true: Lola called, she's at the bar with the girls, they miss you, they're waiting for you. Or else she'd leave a bottle of red wine on the table. But Juan wouldn't overdo it: any distraction could make him lose his edge and the perfect censor had to be alert, keen, attentive, and sharp to nab cheats. He had a truly patriotic task, both self-denying and uplifting.

His basket for censored letters became the best fed as well as the most cunning basket in the whole *Censorship Division*. He was about to congratulate himself for having finally discovered his true mission, when his letter to Mariana reached his hands. Naturally, he censored it without regret. And just as naturally, he couldn't stop them from executing him the following morning, another victim of his devotion to his work.

tr. David Unger

· *Open Door*

The Snow White

Watchman

In the back, behind glass, there are flowers and ferns like in a huge box. And here in front, also in a glass box (bulletproof), is the security guard, who has something in common with the plants, a certain secret that comes to him from the earth. And between one glass cage and the other, the young, prematurely aged junior executives, so elegant in their impeccable suits and precise smiles. It is true that they are rather less aloof than the guard, but, as young junior executives of a financial institution, they are not trained to kill and this makes them a bit less circumspect. Not too much. Hardly enough to allow others the freedom of imagining themselves—as our security guard is wont to—making love on the carpet. In unison, mind you, to the syncopated rhythm of the electronic calculators. Beneath them, the secretaries are somehow sadly beautiful, nearly all of them light-eyed, and the guard contemplates them with more than a bit of lust and thinks that those blond junior executives—nearly all of them limpid-eyed as well—are in a better position than he to seduce the young secretaries. Except that he has a gun and also—hidden in a briefcase—a telescopic sight and a silencer of the best foreign manufacture. In one inside pocket of his jacket he has his permit to carry weapons, the license that accredits him as a guardian of public order. In the other pocket, who knows what he carries; he doesn't really want to know himself: once he found a lipstick and ended up getting red stains that looked like blood all over his hands. Another time, it was seeds, unidentifiable ones. On one occasion, his hand just seemed to get lost in his pocket lint, among crumbs of tobacco and some other kind of leaves, and now he prefers not to think at all about that pocket while he stands guard over the clients who come and go from the vast offices. He knows that the junior executives may have light eyes, but his glass case has three round eyes (one on each exposed side; the fourth rests against a wall) and they're much more unusual, not to mention more practical and ultimately lethal. From there, he can shoot whoever asks for it and feel secure: this box is his mother and it bears him.

From his glass box, he watches the most whimsical people go by: those with the faces of dwarfs, for example, or women whose shapes violate all laws of aesthetics, or little girls with hair dyed the color of egg yolks. There are times our guard thinks the Company must have these people on contract in order to highlight the physical beauty of the employees, but he always dismisses the idea: this is a financial institution, which exists to make money, not to waste it on outlandish schemes.

And he? What is he there for? He's there to protect the money. And to water the plants, if they would let him.

If only he could go over to that other box from time to time, the one in the back. It is much larger than his, even if it's not bulletproof, it is airier, and the step from watching over the bread to watching over the flower isn't that great if you're liberal with your puns. It's a step that would make him very

· *Open Door*

happy, especially since all the money belongs to others—it can never be his—while the plants belong to no one in particular. They have their own lives, and he could water them, fondle them, even talk to them softly as if they were a friendly dog, like that fellow who spent his days taking care of his own with the greatest tenderness—of a wolfdog and a carnivorous plant. He doesn't have to love that much in order to kill people. He doesn't even have to care about the office workers, although he is there to defend them, to lay down his life for them. Except nothing ever happens: nobody menacing ever walks in, nobody attempts a robbery. Sometimes a suspicious package on a bench attracts his attention, but the person who forgot it returns immediately and goes off cheerfully with the misplaced package under his arm. So, if there is a bomb in the package, it will blow up far from the sacrosanct office. And a security guard's duty is to defend the Company, not the entire city, much less the universe. His duty is merely that: act in defense, never in attack, although if he had half a brain he would know the possible aggressor might well be one of his own kind and not something utterly alien to him, like the safe.

But my life won't come cheap, he says to himself sometimes, repeating the phrase so often heard during training, without realizing that every mortal thinks the same thing, with or without the law's permission (life is not something to be given up just like that, much less one's own life, but he has a license to kill and feels at ease). So he sleeps peacefully at night when not on duty, and he sometimes dreams of those plants in the back, when he's not dreaming about the pretty, naked secretaries, a bit stiff, but always exciting. Dreams that are really daydreams, fantasies in which the Company's handsome employees entwine naked on the carpet that muffles the sound of their movements. The carpet as silencer. There in his crystal box—Snow White, goddammit!—he too has a pistol with a silencer and also stands silent as a plant. Almost vegetable, really. Silent there in his glass cage, caressing his silencer while he imagines those outside in positions completely beyond the limits of respectability.

So there he is, summed up in his fantasies, defending with his very humanity what doesn't in the least belong to him. Not even remotely. A perfectly moronic life. Defending what? The vault, the honor of the secretaries, that secure air of the executives, junior executives, and the rest of the employees (their elegant presence). Defending the customers. Defending other people's dough.

That thought occurred to him one fine day. The following day, he forgot it. A week later, he remembered, and after that, little by little, it rooted itself ever more firmly in his brain. A touch of humanity after all, the spark of an idea. Something that was being born, warm as his fondness for those plants in the back. Something called resentment.

He began to go to work dragging his feet. Now he didn't feel like such a big man any more. He no longer dreamt there in front of the mirror that his was a calling only for the brave.

What a revelation, the day he knew (deep inside, in a place he never realized existed) that his calling for the brave was a calling for dipshits, that showing you had balls didn't necessarily mean putting them on the line in defense of others. It was as if someone had given him the famous kiss on his sleeping forehead, as if he had awakened, illuminated.

These were all things impossible to communicate to his superiors. But he was used to keeping his mouth shut, to keeping to himself like a treasure those limited feelings that had grown slowly inside him over the course of his life. Not many— merely vague notions that things were going on within him in spite of himself. And having endured without a word that long, bodily torment called training, how could he sit down now with his superiors—and who could dream of sitting in

· *Open Door*

their presence?—and expound on his doubts or voice his complaints.

So it was that, little by little, he began to nurse a clarifying resentment. He now spent entire afternoons in his glass case concentrating on something more concrete than his erotic fantasies. He stopped imagining the young executives rolling around with the secretaries on the carpet and began to see them for what they really were, each one fulfilling his specific duties. Coming and going in respectful silence, astutely manipulating money, shares, bonds, letters of credit, foreign currency. And they were all so insultingly young, attractive.

It was good for a few months to strip those bodies of all their auras and see them solely in their function as workers. Our security guard became realistic, systematic. He began to come out of his cage and stroll through those rooms seeded with desks; he started to exchange a few words with the more accessible employees; he smiled at the secretaries, had long chats with one of the brokers from the stock exchange. He became an intimate of the doorman. He got around to mentioning to a few of them his fondness for the plants and, at some point when he noticed they were a bit withered, asked if he might water them after hours. Locking up, the others got accustomed to leaving him behind, taking care of the plants—spraying them, dusting the soot off them so they could breathe better.

One evening he gave full rein to his passion and spent two hours among the plants, sipping maté. The night watchman felt he had no choice but to mention the incident to his superiors, and everyone was afraid that the security guard was turning into a poet, most certainly deleterious to someone in his line of work. But there was no reason to fear. His vigilance was as conscientious as ever, and indeed, he showed himself quite active in his hours on duty. He even foiled a dangerous robbery thanks to his fast reflexes and intuition, something his bosses all praised. He knew how to accept his recompense with absolute dignity, aware he had done nothing more than protect his own interests. His superiors in security and the Company directors in attendance at the simple ceremony saw the guard's humility as a noble sentiment, a real satisfaction at duty fulfilled. They doubled his reward then and there, and returned to their respective homes with the calming assurance that the financial institution enjoyed absolute unbeatable security.

Thanks to the doubled reward, the guard outfitted himself as he needed and had only to wait, putting into practice the patience he had learned from the plants. When finally he felt the moment had arrived, he struck with such efficiency that it was impossible to follow his trail or discover his whereabouts. That is, in the eyes of the others, he achieved his old dream: the earth swallowed him up.

tr. Christopher Leland

· Open Door

Cat's Eye

I.

They are walking down the hallway in the dark. She turns
around suddenly and he cries out. "What is it?" she asks. And
he says: "Your eyes. Your eyes are shining like a wild animal's."

"Oh, come on," she says, "look again." And nothing, of
course. She turns to him and there's nothing but pure, calming
darkness. He puts his hand on the switch and turns on the
light. She has her eyes closed. She closed them against the
light, he thinks, but that really doesn't put his mind at rest.

The dialogue between the two of them changes after that vision of phosphorescence in her eyes. Green eyes casting their
own light, now so brown, hazel as her ID says; brown or hazel,
that is, conventional there in the everyday light of the office.
He had planned to propose a job to her, and a green phosphorescence had imposed itself between the two of them (*ignis fa-
tuus*). Outside is the Calle Corrientes, so edificed and unedify-
ing. Inside the office, jungle noises conjured up by a pair of
shining eyes. Okay, okay, starting like this, we'll never know

how our objective narrative of events comes out. The window is open. We want to note the fact that the window is open to somehow explain the jungle noises, although if noise can be explained by noise, the light in her eyes in the hallway has no rational explanation on account of the closed door between the open window and the reigning darkness.

That she turned toward him in the hall—that's undeniable. And afterward, those glowing eyes—to what end were they looking at him? With what threat or demand? If he hadn't cried out . . . ? On the fourteenth floor, in the office, he asks himself these questions while he talks to her—talks to a pair of eyes—and he doesn't know very well what he'll be saying in the next instant, what's expected of him and where is—was—the trap into which he has slowly slid. Tiger's eyes. He asks himself as he talks with her with the open window behind them: If he had been able to stifle the cry or intuit something more . . .

II.

At three in the morning a suspicious noise awakens you and you remain very quiet in bed and hear—sense—that someone is moving there in your room. Some man. A man who has forced the door; who surely now wants to force himself on you. You hear his velvet footsteps over the carpet and feel a light vibration in the air. The man is getting closer. You don't dare move. Suddenly, within you, there is something beyond terror—or is it terror itself?—and you turn in the darkness and confront him. On seeing what you suppose is the glow of your eyes, the guy lets out a shriek and jumps through the window, which, since it's a hot night, is wide open. Among other things, two questions now arise:

    a) Are you the same woman as the one in the previous story?
    b) How will you explain the presence of the man in your house when the police begin their investigation?

· *Open Door*

Answer to a

Yes, you are the same woman as in the previous story. For this reason, and bearing in mind the foregoing events, you wait until 9:00 A.M. and go running to consult an ophthalmologist. The doctor, a conscientious professional, puts you through all manner of examinations and finds nothing abnormal about your vision. It's not really your vision that's the problem, you suggest without going into detail. The doctor then scans your retinas, and discovers a black panther in the depths of your eyes. He doesn't know how to explain this phenomenon to you. He can only inform you of the fact and leave the explanation to wiser or more imaginative colleagues. You return to your house stunned, and to calm down you begin to tweeze some hairs from your upper lip. Inside you, the panther roars, but you don't hear her.

The answer to b) is unknown

Green eyes of a black panther, phosphorescent in the darkness, unreflected in mirrors as might have been expected from the very beginning, had there been a beginning. The man from the first story is now her boss and, of course, has no desire to give her orders for fear that she'll suddenly turn out the lights and make him face those eyes again. Luckily for him, the panther doesn't lurk elsewhere in her, and the days go by with that peculiar placidity associated with the habit of fear. The man takes certain precautions every morning. Before leaving for the office, he makes sure the electric company has no plans to cut the power in the neighborhood. He keeps a flashlight within easy reach in the top drawer of his desk, leaves the window wide open so even the last shimmer of day can enter, and does not permit himself even a hint of darker sentiments toward her as he has permitted himself toward previous secretaries. Not that he wouldn't like that. He would like to take her dancing some night and then to bed. But the terror of facing those eyes again doesn't even allow him to entertain the notion. All he permits himself is to wonder whether he really saw what he thinks he saw or if it was merely the product of his imagination (an optical illusion of someone else's eye). He decides on for the first alternative, because he can't believe his imagination is that fecund. To keep her docile, he speaks to her in musical tones, though she doesn't appear to be stalking him as she takes dictation.

Buenos Aires cannot permit itself—cannot permit him—the luxury of a conscious hallucination. We who have known him for some time can be sure that his fear has nothing to do with the imaginative. We are not that fond of him, but we'll see if, with time, we'll give him the opportunity to redeem himself. Nor is she any big deal either. It's the panther that saves her, but a panther like this one, *che non parla ma se fica*, doesn't have much of a chance inside someone so given to apathy. She begins to suffer from darkaphobia or whatever they call it, and she only frequents well-lighted places so no one will find out her useless secrets. The panther sleeps with open eyes while she's awake; perhaps it is awake while she's asleep, but she's never able to ascertain that. The panther needs no food, nor any kind of affection. The panther is now called Pepita, but that's about all. The boss begins to look upon her favorably, but never looks her in the eyes. She and the boss wind up together in broad daylight on the office carpet. Their relationship lasts quite a while.

The denouement is optional:

—Once a year, Pepita goes into heat. The boss does what he can, but the woman remains cockeyed.

· *Open Door*

—She ends up pushing the boss out the window because the eyes are the window of the soul and vice versa.

—Pepita moves from the eyes to the liver and the woman dies of cirrhosis.

—She and the boss decide to get married and their light bills are incredible because they don't ever want to be in the dark.

—Pepita begins to misbehave, and the woman finds herself forced to leave her beloved and go to live with an animal trainer who mistreats her.

—Ditto, but with an ophthalmologist who promises her an operation.

—Ditto, but with a veterinarian because Pepita is sick and the woman is afraid of going blind if the panther dies.

—Every day the woman washes her eyes with Lotus Flower Eye Bath and is very serene because Pepita has converted to Buddhism and practices nonviolence.

—She reads that in the United States they have discovered a new method of combatting black panthers, and she travels, full of hope, only to find, once there, that the reference was to something completely different.

—She leaves the boss due to his insalubrious habit of screwing in bright light and she plugs herself into a job as an usherette in a ritzy movie theater where everyone appreciates the fact that she has no need for a flashlight.

tr. Christopher Leland

Flea

Market

First, the trees in the plaza began to drop their leaves. That left exposed the broad square of cement that from the balconies overhead must look like a patio carpeted with dry leaves. So, out of season, the summer only just begun, and the leaves falling long before their time. From trees that have turned in order to be different from the trees in the other plazas. Miserable trees, absolutely miserly. They did it just to keep from giving us shade on Sundays and Holy Days, when we convene in the plaza/adorn the plaza/adore the plaza. Because our mission there is not limited to stringing it with tinsel; we fill that tiny plaza with colors, odors, sounds; we burn incense in it and our music overflows it, though not strictly in its honor—tiny little lazy, grayish, square, simple plaza—but to lure buyers, because they haven't been coming the way they used to. The worst of all fates, no buyers. They've been driven away by the lack of protection from the sizzling sun, the absence of a

· *Open Door*

breeze. Not a breath of air anywhere, though you can't blame that on the fallen leaves so much as on the stubborn absence of the buyers themselves—it was their coming and going that created the refreshing breeze. Yes, the air moved as the buyers wandered from stall to stall, admiring an ancient bowl, dickering about a prize, fingering and leafing through incunabula and ancient sheets of music, trying on a Manila shawl, laughing before a small art deco statue, buying, yes, almost always buying something that would enable one of us to get through an August, which in this part of the world falls—used to fall— at the end of the year.

Second-Floor View

The gypsies have been observing them from the balconies that hang almost directly over the plaza. The gypsies have been watching how the luck has turned for those below who on a day in mid-spring decided to imitate them. Imitate gypsies! Lords of barter, masters of copper—who could imagine such insolence?

Reflective behind their half-doors, the gypsies have seen the leaves falling from the trees as if it were autumn, though it is scarcely the beginning of summer. This is happening to those below because they tried to be something they weren't, because they dressed in clothing of colors not even slightly in harmony with the grayness of their lives.

The Little Plaza

It is square, with beautiful trees given to losing their leaves, and more or less framed by two streets. Half a block. Balconied two-story houses with a nostalgia for the past surround the plaza. No one realizes that the gypsies have been occupying the

upper stories in order to secretly observe those below. Those below, while lamenting the inexplicable absence of buyers, never look up.

On Sundays and Holy Days the fair is again reassembled in the plaza. The flea market. But for no one. Except for the increasingly melancholy merchants, and the gypsies above, who, unknown to anyone, play muted tambourines. Those who normally would be clients are taking refuge in the churches on Sunday mornings, and in the afternoons they go to the movies. They no longer come to the little plaza, or wander through the neighboring streets. The colors in the plaza are sterile colors. If those below do not do something soon, the colors will fade away and blend into the gray paving stones and scaling tree trunks.

Upstairs, the gypsies dance amid swirling gauze.

Below, the merchants maintain their somber simulation of happiness.

Upstairs, the gypsies burn herbs; below, the merchants, waiting for some buyer to happen by, feel fear creeping nearer.

And so it is on Sundays.

On weekdays, the little plaza recaptures its summer face, the leaves again clothe the trees, and small boys play ball, old men weave their cloth of memories, women knit theirs, someone brings the parrot cage outside to air.

Ground-Floor View

And what about this Sunday? A ray of hope in the form of a dark-skinned young girl. A girl, scarcely clothed, with a blazing mane of hair. We loved her immediately; hers was the only new face we had seen during all those too-long weeks. I think she came from one of the houses surrounding the little plaza. I gave her a ring; I was the first. Then others gave her bracelets, a silvered belt, ropes of necklaces, beads, brooches, and

· *Open Door*

pins; by noontime she even had ankle bracelets. With her olive skin, she was a living jewel. People kept adding more and more brightly colored skirts, an embroidered blouse, a heavy lace shawl with silk fringe.

Thus adorned, the girl lifted her head and smiled upward—from the distance you could hear laughter. The girl turned her neck with incomparable grace, and from above came the sound of something like applause. She wanted to dance among the stalls of the fair, but this was difficult under the weight of the gifts she had been given. She wanted to sing, but her throat was so choked with necklaces she couldn't raise her voice.

From somewhere in the depths of the houses came a sound of alarm. A cry of anguish. The girl made a movement as if to run away but something held her back; maybe she had become entangled in one of her many long skirts or perhaps her shawl was caught or someone took her by the arm—or all these things together. She stood in the sunlight in the exact center of the plaza, receiving our love. We wanted to hold her at any cost, because she had come to save us. That's why we surged toward her from all four corners of the plaza. They are going to say now that we wanted to entrap her, but that isn't true. We were pushing closer only to touch her and hug her. Closer and closer, pressing closer because we loved her so much, because she could save us. We didn't mean to choke her. No one is going to believe us.

tr. Margaret Sayers Peden

Legend

of the

Self-Sufficient

Child

"The way he shuffles the deck isn't manly. He's worse than a faggot. He's like a woman. Disgusting," remark the peasants as they play cards at night in the tavern.

"She looks at us like a man would. She must be a man dressed up like a woman to get near us. We shouldn't put up with something so wicked," the women remark in the morning in the general store.

The place is the same. Is it the same person?

A man who is a woman, a woman who's a man, or both at a time, interchangeable.

Poor little town. So much doubt, such metaphysical anguish even if it can't be expressed exactly . . . Town? Ha! Twenty or so houses, spread out and low slung so as not to offend the pampas, an abandoned church. A very few said to themselves: Oh, if the padre were still alive, he'd help us figure out this mystery, he'd protect us. Most people decided to follow their own instincts and watch this strange being closely,

· Open Door

yes, though not *too* closely, to avoid falling into the black pit of contagion.

In the town, one can see, there are no natives, most have Italian blood, there are a couple of Englishmen who don't take sides (the gaucho has long left but the devil remains). A gaucho would have known how to interpret the secrets in the whinnies of his own horse when this undefinable creature drew close to the hitching post. (The townspeople understand very little about horses: they tie them to posts and then don't give the poor animals a second thought as if, on the pampas, you shouldn't always carry your horse close to your heart, even at a distance or indoors.) As for this creature, it has neither horse nor dog—of course not: animals sense the smell of the devil no matter how deep the devil hides himself.

At the first light of dawn, does this person scrape off his manhood to cast off the devil? And put it back on at nightfall for fear of having the devil bottled up in a jar?

Or does this endemoned creature really belong to the female sex? Does the devil get in when she's a woman, having sprouted breasts and bearing milk? Or is the Evil One always there, running up and down from breasts to balls for the sheer pleasure of traveling? Traveling on a schedule just like the bus that grinds down the dusty highway every Tuesday afternoon. But the Evil One is never delayed: with the evening star he becomes a man and wanders around all night like the town crier. Sometimes, people have seen him hunker down in the tall grass and sleep till the dew falls; then, as dawn approaches, return to his wagon and—in the blink of an eye—emerge changed into a woman.

As night falls, these matters are discussed at the bar while the stranger leans on the counter a prudent distance away. Under that friendly roof, with the heat of gin upon them, the townspeople feel a certain brotherhood, free to talk about that person who, beneath the open sky, does things that make them tremble at the sacrilege. The barkeep doesn't take part in all the conjecturing, the jokes and perturbation. He knows that one double client equals two clients. Two customers come out of that strange wagon, and that's the only important thing. The devil does not enter into his calculations.

As for the wagon, that's a story in itself. Early one morning, the farmers saw it sitting on the communal lands. They could not explain how it got there, though they frankly didn't think much about it. Not that one often saw a wagon parked a league outside of town, but it was so humble—a golden, toast color like the earth itself—in those thistle-covered fields beneath an azure sky. It possessed a certain heraldic air that stirred some ancestral strain in the farmer's blood. Nobody objected to it. Not long afterward, however, the peculiarity of the wagon's inhabitant was discovered, and at that point the talk about witchcraft and fear started to spread through the streets of the town, and it was good to feel it breaking the tranquility. Distrust ran right alongside fear, but distrust was an old friend and really didn't disturb anyone.

And now, the second verse.

Not even the best yarnspinner could hold it against this story, simple as it is, and unpretentious.

She is María José and he is José María, two persons in one, each of them, if you think in terms of names, but absolutely unrelated to the idea the others have come up with that amalgamates the two of them in one being. Something profoundly religious. Inconfessable.

They are two, I repeat: José María and María José, born of the same womb on the same morning, perhaps a bit mixed up.

And the years went by for them, too, till they reached this point where a vast assortment of impossibilities began to

· *Open Door*

weigh on them, over and above the desire to do as they wish. They can't just go on: they're stuck in the mud and out of gas. They can't even split up because the fear of one without the other becomes unbearable. At the same time, they can't sleep together for fear of that evil entanglement everybody knows about, the taboo of the species being contrary to the interest of the species.

He goes out at night, makes the darkness his own. She goes out in the daylight, as long as it lasts, and neither of the two cuts the cord, stays away any longer than necessary from the wagon, that womb on wheels. (And to think that they were so close, packed tight together, when they began this life, and now they can't touch each other or even look at each other for that visceral fear of temptation.)

(*In those times before we were born, was yours the arm that clasped my body? From whom came that all-embracing pleasure, that placenta?*)

Now, without realizing it, he has begun to acquire the feline grace that is hers, and she has started to become firmer in her gestures and perhaps—who would deny it?—looks with longing at the women of the town, the only people who cross her diurnal path while the men are in the fields, eating up the earth with their tractors, or taking care of the cattle (work appropriate to this rough continent, with its feet and hands and even its soul in the earth). And he, by night, perhaps nearly despairs in his desire to reach his own soft hand out and touch one of those calloused hands that know of the knife and the raw flesh.

And every minute those hands pull farther away, and the town is more united against them, not letting them speak, not letting them explain.

It seems to me that in all of life's little dramas, it is useful to place the blame on somebody. Our scapegoat will be that long-lost priest who named the two babies. The soutane, of course, distanced him from much sexual knowledge, but it really is unpardonable. He should have taken a better look: the one, María María, and the other, José José, and that would have ruled out doubts. Not all such inquiries are salacious; sometimes they are scientific.

Chorus

"That man is a woman in drag. She is hiding something even without trying."

"That woman's a man, and he'll throw himself all over us if we give him half a chance."

No clear definition for them, poor things, and never a smile. It is all too much. After six days, on a Friday night, to be precise, José María can not gather the strength to move his body across the fields toward a comforting drink. He leaves María José almost the whole bed at first. But within a short time, things begin to get tangled: there it is, within the reach of a hand and of other anatomical parts, that long longed warmth. There; the caring and the hope, the return to the source, and so much more that it is best not to mention in case there are minors around. And there are: after the prescribed time a child was born, very beautiful and utterly sexless, absolutely smooth, though over the years it developed quite differently, with peaks and valleys, with an intriguing bulk and a dark cavity of notable depth.

Outside the wagon, no one ever knew which of the two had been the mother.

Did they know themselves?

tr. Christopher Leland

· *Open Door*

Country

Carnival

When Eulalia saw him leaving the barn, heading toward the dance hall, she couldn't contain her disgust and she shouted after him, "Surrealist!" She wasn't exactly sure what the word meant, but she suspected that it was just right for something all different colors without rhyme or reason like the cockatoo at the general store. Ermenegildo had thought he'd dressed up in motley, but now he knew better because of Eulalia, and when his friend asked him what he was dressed as he answered without the slightest hesitation, "A surrealist."

There were more than a few remarks made along the way before they got to the dance hall. Once they were there, Ermenegildo and his friend stopped at the entrance so everyone could have a look at them and so they could scout things out a bit. It wasn't that the girls were skittish that sultry night, so full of bugs. Gnats that sting and of the other kind: the ones who buzz around the girls without letting them catch their breath, to the point that the girls tilt their heads a little, as if those human insects were at their beck and call, ready to shake their bones with whoever was at hand.

Only a few in costume. Every carnival, it was the same, and Erme should have known better but, well, the temptation to make a splash had been too great and almost without thinking he had thrown on every colorful rag he could find in the shack, and he'd ended up dressed like a surrealist. Pretty surprising.

On the dance floor they were beginning to kick up some dust, and the two men went on scouting, disinclined to pay the admission fee if they were only going to end up wallflowers. The girls were getting pickier by the minute and you had to ask yourself why they came to the dance in the first place, because whenever some poor sap nodded to them they acted like they didn't understand and the fellow wound up embarrassed in the back of the shed, droopy-eared as a hound just pulled out of a well. Except, of course, the sap stayed down in the well, that deep hole that shapes itself around somebody who's all alone. A sad state of affairs, my friend, but Erme, dressed in all the colors of the rainbow, simply couldn't be sad or droopy-eared. He had to bust into the dance, his head held high with his cap on top and the pride of being one of the few people in costume in the whole place. So he came laughing onto the floor, something the girls seemed to like, just as they liked seeing him colorful as a cockatoo, shimmering among those pathetic clod-hoppers in their black hats with kerchiefs around their necks.

The girls laughed, Ermenegildo laughed louder. If only Eulalia could have seen him, she would die of spite. The girls laughed with him, not at him like somebody else we could mention, and Erme took advantage of this by nodding at the snootiest of all the girls, so snooty she looked prudish. She accepted his invitation by barely tilting her head and raising her eyebrows, but she didn't move from her seat. In a jiffy, he was next to her and, as the polka started, not knowing what to talk to her about, he asked her her name.

· *Open Door*

"I'll tell you if you'll tell me first, what are you dressed up as?"

"As a surrealist."

"That sounds impressive. What is it?"

"A surrealist? A surrealist . . . is a soldier from another time, when being a soldier was something merry."

"And brave."

"Of course."

"And beautiful."

"Uh-huh."

"And tender."

"If you say so . . ."

They danced the polka; they danced the *chamamé* till they almost dropped, and Erme was not the type that dropped easily. And she wasn't either. They sweated a lot during the dance like you're supposed to, and she, in the meantime, forgot to tell him her name. But during one of the intervals that evening, she said to him.

"Surrealist. Forward march. Let's go home."

"To your house?"

"Of course. Where else? I wouldn't be going to yours. I'm a decent girl."

Something any good surrealist ought to understand, Erme told himself, and so they set out on the road beneath the moon and through the countryside until they got to the army barracks.

"Halt! Who goes there?" A stern voice demanded.

"It's your daughter," Miss Prude replied, and Erme nearly had a heart attack. Even more so when that stern voice opened the gate and pulled them inside.

"And what's this?"

"He's a surrealist, Father."

"Looks like a cockatoo to me."

"No, Father, you're mistaken. He's a surrealist, a soldier

from the time when being a soldier was something merry and brave and tender."

"Not these days."

"Not these days, no, Father. You know that very well."

"Well, you, my girl, should know that your father is always up to a good thrashing."

"This man is merry, Father."

"And I'll merrily let him have it."

"This man is brave."

"Brave? This I want to see."

"And tender."

"That I won't give him a chance to show us."

And, steaming, he went after Erme with a strap, and the poor fellow ended up like a mishatched parrot, half-plucked, just a rag. Though a colorful one.

The two men finally stood face-to-face. The barracks commander had lost his breath, but poor Ermenegildo had lost his spirit. The spirit of the carnival, at least, and all for a girl who, when it came down to it, really wasn't that pretty, just prudish, and sly to boot. The silliness of the situation finally got to him, and he let out a guffaw there in the midst of all the hullabaloo.

"A surrealist doesn't laugh, he defends himself," Little Miss Prude spat.

"Laughter's the best defense."

To go to dance and come out lashed; to go for wool and come out shorn. Only come out wasn't the right word, because he had to stay for a year there at the barracks wearing fatigues. One more raw recruit.

Little Miss Prude walked among the troops, passing out words of encouragement as if they were orders, although with the surrealist everything was so topsy-turvy that even orders turned to honey in her mouth, and drew flies. So it was that Ermenegildo went along with his recruitment without rebelling: not for the orders or the flies but for the honey that covered everything and gave it a golden shimmer. He remained,

· *Open Door*

and ended up doing the most unexpected tasks: chopping wood for the entire regiment or spending whole days on maneuvers. The training was constant. Leapfrog; drop-drill; target practice; wrestling. Every so often, in the midst of his most extreme exertion—like the time they were clearing the thicket—the smile of Little Miss Prude would appear and Erme would find new strength. It was true, of course, that there were long periods when he missed the barn and the cow Aurora more than any other one and he even thought fondly of Eulalia, without considering it might be her fault that he was in this mess.

There are things a Christian doesn't rail against. And so he just went on—hup, two, three—there in the service, until war broke out and he was sent to the front in recognition of his courage. Courage? Indeed. It all began with a little set-to among the troops. It seems that El Negro Morón was making eyes—really making eyes—at Little Miss Prude, and our poor Ermenegildo simply blew up. His long military training had made him strong and tough, and he was able to beat El Negro Morón in single combat. This unexpected triumph established his prestige among the troops and earned him a commission when the war broke out.

The fighting lasted several months, and it wasn't as easy as it was believed at first: the enemy knew how to vanish into the jungle so well that the jungle itself became the enemy. Which is the reason our good old Ermenegildo didn't even have time to pine for anything. Only during the moments he was setting up a bivouac or digging a trench could he sigh for those old times when to be a soldier was something merry, or at least safe. Brave and tender, Miss Prude had added that night long ago when misfortune began to befall him. Miss Prude: she stayed behind at the barracks patching the colorful costume, washing it and ironing it so he might someday recapture that first day, when Eulalia yelled after him. What was it Eulalia had shouted? Surrealist, she had yelled at him so long ago, and he had believed her and a surrealist he would be until the day he died.

But phooey on death. He only had to last out the war—fighting—and then return to the barracks covered in glory. His bravery in every moment on the front finally brought him a night of love with Little Miss Prude—the best reward—and a medal awarded by her father in front of the entire regiment.

There was a long speech by the commander in which he spoke of Ermenegildo's military valor. He lauded his strategy, he mentioned that day when he saw him arrive dressed in many colors and chicken-hearted. He expounded upon the merits of military life, which in barely a year turned cream puffs into warriors. He sang the praises of physical training and the discipline of barracks life. He did not speak of love but, at the end of his long harangue, he declared: "Private Ermenegildo, in recognition of your meritorious service in time of war, you may ask of me what you will" and he looked at him like a father-in-law.

Erme either misunderstood or pretended to, and he asked only that his suit of colors be returned to him and that he be released from any further service. There was no alternative but to do the hero's will, and everyone bade him farewell with tears in their eyes. Little Miss Prude in the first place.

And off he went at a comfortable pace and the road to the farm was a long one and he had to walk all night by the light of the moon and he arrived long after the first rays of dawn.

When she saw him, still far off, Eulalia yelled: "You bum!" And as he got closer, she added: "So you think this is a decent hour to get back, still dressed like a circus clown since Saturday night? Why haven't you changed? And what do you mean, leaving me here all day Sunday without showing your face? And to make things worse, you've got that medal slung around your neck. You jackass."

tr. Christopher Leland

· Open Door

Generous

Impediments

Float

Downriver

Dark, glossy impediments, like snakeskins a bit tattered in their uselessness. The whole snake—a snakeskin full of itself—would be just the opposite, a ringing voice of alarm.

What now floats downriver, unsettling everyone, is subtler, clinging to the huge tangled reeds, almost like words. That is, they are messages; they are disasters. Disasters? The messages? No doubt about it. You have to be able to appreciate them in all their glory, and the sunlight must be just right so a stray beam does not alter their meaning.

In any case, the messages float downriver and the whole city congregates on the banks and spends the afternoon watching them, hoping for a little enlightenment.

(Those who can expect real benefits are the ones vending sodas along the banks. Those who enjoy some secret benefit are the rare folk who have always conversed with the river and understand its language.) The others just stand there, swigging their soft drinks (all of them traitors to water) and, after

passing entire days trying to decipher the water lilies, complain about the interference (a snakeskin, the bitten-off tail of
an iguana). The river is like that. It doesn't aim to please
anybody. It is very wide and calm and murky and when it gets
its back up, it is not always kind. It is subtle and sibylline and
comes from far away where it does as it chooses (snaking in
meanders that finally join in rings of water with islands at their
hearts. It runs in rapids, leaps in waterfalls, slowly wears away
stone and even more slowly goes about remaking it elsewhere).
The river does its work as it has since time immemorial without
anyone getting on its way, and now, suddenly, everybody in the
city is trying to understand it, listening for an oracle. (What
will become of us, of me, of him, of my family? Will the mayor
ever do anything significant? Will he ever stop making
speeches?)

If the river is telling them something (which it likely is; it is
never selfish), it should be sufficient to know the river to know
everything about it and await its flooding like a revelation. Wait
and hope without building up too many illusions, as if it were
merely habit, until that particular afternoon when somebody
shouted *the Messiah*. One of these days, somebody said, the
Messiah will arrive, swept along by the waters, and we must
catch him, rescue him, not allow the current to carry him further along to those imbeciles in the city downstream who think
they are so much better than us because they face the delta.

The Messiah will come for us and he'll come singing, others
prophesied. And if we don't hear him? If he passes at a distance? This is a huge river, a powerful one . . . Will he come
on a boat, a raft? Will he come on a tangle of reeds, in a woven
basket like Moses, or astride a log or a fish, a *dorado* most likely,
with shimmering gold scales, seems better suited for him than
anything else. And if he were to pass by under water and we
missed him?

· *Open Door*

It took twenty-seven days and nights for the city to produce the net that would span the river from one bank to the other and reach all the way to the bottom. No one stopped weaving or sewing during this time, and even the terminally ill recovered their strength in order to put in their quota of work. Nobody, absolutely nobody, refused to take part, each one weaving as well as he could: the old ladies crocheting or tatting, the men tying knots and binding together the different pieces—knitted scraps, lace doilies, macramé coverlets, bridal veils, all braided, plaited. The rope-works was left empty of rope; the packers without twine; little girls went without jump ropes, the sheep without wool, and nobody whined about the shortages. During those twenty-seven almost holy days, it didn't occur to anyone to utter the least complaint, and a strange smile from deep inside began to spread across their faces. There were some who took to singing, softly at first, then louder as the net grew larger. They even organized choirs.

And like those spiders that live in the marshes and weave giant, communal webs, they also learned to sleep clustered in the shadows at siesta time, then to wake up and keep working. The net expanded to the point it covered the entire riverbank. That spiderweb.

Many even managed to completely eliminate sleeping at night so they could continue the work that seemed endless: the light of the torches and the silence drew them toward ecstasy. A telegraphy with thread, a tactile communication flourished among them thanks to this net, which would catch the Messiah. Catch the Messiah? No, no. Only signal him of his journey's end, mark on the long course of this river the place that, in all humility, awaited him. A quiet act of contrition, because the Messiah would divvy up a healthy lot of penance, and they, in some way, were looking to expiate their sins.

They reveled in feeling so close in their sins and in taking measures to atone for them. Pleasant to the point of greeting the dawn exhilarated, with stirring hymns, both to welcome the sun and, why deny it, to awaken the sleepyheads.

It did not rain even one of those twenty-seven days. The weather was memorably still. Nobody died, nor was anyone born: there were no distractions. There was only the weaving—the best possible—and the joining of the fabrics until the measurements were exactly right. After that, all sorts of floats were attached to one side, and weights to the other. Then one of the ends of the net was secured to the most vigorous trees along the bank in preparation for the following day.

That day was truly festive! The town band set out in a passenger launch, and the mayor and his men got on a boat in order to make the towing of the net more ceremonial. Never had the mayor's men rowed so hard, never had they been so tough. It was a historic event. They certainly had never heard such cheers and applause as they did when they arrived on the opposite shore and, with some effort, fastened the free end of the net to other sturdy trees. On this bank, there was a toast and fireworks and even a dance, and when the mayor finally returned, after rowing by the rubber duckies, balls, dolls, and plastic trucks used as floats, he was received as never before and, for the first time, his speech was greeted heartily. The mayor emphasized civic responsibility, as always, but he spoke too of hope, and gradually the citizens recovered their ability to respond to real life: many wept uncontrollably and one old man allowed himself the luxury of dying of an emotion-sparked heart attack.

With the net duly secured, after several hours of celebration, the citizens returned home to recharge their batteries. The reception of the Messiah would require a serene and rested spirit, and hands clear of all impurity so they might touch the Messiah, venerate him. He would come floating

· *Open Door*

downriver, and at the foot of the city he would pause, there within everyone's reach. The Messiah would come from one of those remote countries where the river is born and nothing would block his way till he arrived at their city. Nothing, not even the waterfalls. The Messiah was meant for them, and he would not continue on to the execrable city downriver. What country would he come from? Did it matter?

And while they went along weaving such speculations as they had earlier woven the net, the net itself silently began to do its work. It snagged the abundant tangle of reeds in its threads, caught some floating logs, a dead calf or two, whatever was swept along by the current, things the water washes away and that only the water can recognize after their decomposition (a disintegration with the logical consequence of a complete integration—the two processes inseparable).

The net restrained all the flotsam of the river and the river raced on stripped of its ballast. It ran freely for a short time, but we all know the retentive power of that which we want to discard as useless. Little by little, with no one really noticing, the flotsam caught in the net began to form a dense barrier, a wall from one bank of the river to the other, while the city's citizens dreamt of salvation.

The river's deeds are hushed, and when in the middle of the night the waters rose, they did so silently.

Those first ones up at dawn discovered the disaster and sounded the alarm. Howls of alarm because the river was swelling rapidly and threatened to flood everything.

For so great a desire to retain Him whom the water would bear, all they had managed to retain was the water itself. In the town meeting that lasted half an hour—the situation was so desperate that the mayor couldn't even launch into a short speech—it was unanimously decided that the moorings must be cut to free the river, and so, with this simple act, deprive the city of its messianic illusions. What were they supposed to do? It was surely better to remain dry if humble fishermen than to achieve an amphibious salvation via amphibious avenues.

A few dissident extremists rose up, as always in situations like this, to announce the end of the world by flood, and ran off to seek safety in treetops. The more water they get, the taller the trees grow, they proclaimed, and the safer we'll be.

The mayor didn't even listen to them. He said a few brief, allusive words, and then, followed by his entourage, he set out with determined, splashing strides as far as he could while maintaining some semblance of dignity. At that point, a boat arrived to save them all any further embarrassment, and they managed to row against the current to that point on the bank where, one week before (on a day heavy with auguries), they had fixed the net to the thickest tree trunks. Except that now (Oh, consternation, Oh, confusion), the lines of the net were, quite naturally, under water.

The boatman, after thinking it over, pulled out a machete, but made not the least move to jump into the river. The mayor realized this act of daring was reserved for him, and without saying a word—his constituents were at a considerable distance, watching him from the balconies—he stripped off his clothes and dove in with the machete held high. He managed to achieve his goal: he cut the lines, freeing the net with all the flotsam, and the river in that same instant reclaimed its bed with a resounding belch. The mayor was rescued, stark naked, by those in the city downriver.

Half-drowned as he was, he shone an odd blue, almost iridescent, dazzling. Some water plants were tangled around his neck like garlands, and it seems he had a little silver guppy like a star between his eyes. He had lost the power of speech.

The subsequent iconography showed him cross-legged on the giant round leaf of a Victoria Regia. The people of the city

· *Open Door*

upriver began to worship the miraculous image without suspecting its origin, though finding it vaguely familiar. The long pilgrimages downriver and the slow warming between the old rivals resulted in the construction of a common sanctuary midway between the two cities. The Venerated One had died some time before, of pneumonia. And the river flowed on without further ado.

tr. Christopher Leland

The Redtown

Chronicles

1. *Littleherb*

He arrived in this no-man's town shouldering his bundle. He was tired of towns that belonged to someone, to the others.

The first thing he did was write his name on a rock: one way among many to assert himself and avenge himself on stones. They had made him suffer enough—stones, that is—especially when thrown in his face by unknown hands. The stones' fault? No, of course not. But stone he was familiar with and could avenge himself on confidently, whereas the hand that does the throwing is always anonymous. There are too many anonymous hands in the world, though few shameless enough to throw stones at him, who is usually so unobtrusive.

In this town, luckily, no hands, no feet, nothing human; only red sand, red stone; a town indistinguishable from the mountains and abandoned for years.

"Hello," was the first thing he said to the town in general, but most particularly to one house there on the left, which appeared the coziest. Or at least, the most intact: walls of red stone, the color of the earth, and an absolute, spacious roof-lessness that allowed him to see stars in a new, nonmetaphorical way. He dragged his bundle into that new home and settled in. He unrolled his sleeping bag and pulled out his little burner and pot, his gourd and his sipper.

Stingily preparing his maté, he said to himself: "Here I am." And he had never been so much there as in this town that belonged to no one, that was his alone.

The maté had a different flavor, though it was made with the herb from the towns where they had stoned him. He had little left. Littleherb, he called himself, which sounded much sweeter to him than his old name, now abandoned forever on that rock on the outskirts of town.

Stripped of his name, with only Littleherb to cover him, he felt much better—relieved, more in tune with the air of the town. He put more wood on the fire he had built, making a huge blaze inside the house, and he was glad there was neither roof nor door nor anything else combustible around.

Next morning he made a trip through the town, taking possession of places by putting up signs. With that in mind, he had not burned the wood that seemed most likely to be useful, planks on which he could write (for example) "Sheriff's Office" or "Hotel," "Church" or "Town Hall."

But the following day, the sun's first rays hadn't even waked him when the Indians, come down from the highlands, did. He saw them, a stain of color on the red town in their ponchos with geometric designs. To speak with him, they respectfully removed their hats.

"Pardon us, sir, but you can't build a fire here. There can be no life in this town."

"Why not?" he asked, astonished.

And they replied: "Because this is a dead town."

And he had to accept that, whether he liked it or not, because they refused to say anymore and, turning away, left him with that gentle advice that was almost a threat.

"Dead town, my ass," he said to himself. He mumbled a number of other things as he went from door to door nailing up his signs with growing enthusiasm, as if he were resuscitating the town. The noise of hammering made the adobe ring in a new way, and the old walls waggled like the tail of a grateful dog. Later, with the houses marked—posted—it was as if there were people around. "Bakery"—just imagine, there among the rocks—"General Store." "Saloon." "Jail" he never put up, it was too painful for him.

Littleherb went into each building—some almost completely in ruins—and went through a private ritual: "Do come in, ma'am," he would say to a passing breeze, "we have the best merchandise in these parts. What was it you were looking for?"

Dead town. Ha! He, Littleherb, knew it wasn't Deadtown. No! Redtown. Vital, radiant there in the sunshine. A little dry, true. Like the skin of a snake, which was the only animal he had seen during his long wanderings through the town. Not a bird. Not an ant. Nothing. So much the better, he said to himself, no need to worry about spiders crawling into his sleeping bag. But it wasn't very pleasant to find himself like that, with no company at all. A nothing town with nobody in it, only a tiny stream that ran some distance away, without even a fish in the water.

Littleherb was counting on the Indians to help him get a bit of food, but after that first day, they did not come down again. Occasionally, at night, Littleherb thought he heard their voices descending from on high: "Dead town! Dead town!" But they did not venture into the valley.

And Littleherb, involved in reviving the town, didn't notice how he was beginning to resemble it: red and dry. Red from the dust that settled into his pores; dry from that unforgiving

· *Open Door*

sun. Poor Littleherb. He was Hardly-any-herb these days.
Just stubble. Still and all, he continued drinking his maté,
each time a little weaker, and thus passed days that seemed
years to him, as he learned to be happy for long periods. He
finally came to know how to lean quietly against an adobe wall
and allow happiness slowly to infuse him. Happy while he contemplated the distinct tones of the red mountains or when he
put up new and fantastic signs: "Dreameria," "Rainbow
Shop," "Bordello de luxe," "Pink Corner." Happy as he wandered down those deserted desert streets. He didn't even hear
the shouts of "dead town" that those up above cast down on
him, or he thought they cast down. Shouts, after all, don't
hurt, do they? Not like the stones he had been pelted with
when he passed through living towns with his angelic, irritat-
ing air.

He wandered through the red town posting signs, and one
night he slept in the town hall, and the next in the general store,
the bordello, or the bakery. Happy each night, happy in his
days of sign-posting, a happiness ever more solid, even if he
was running out of paint.

Just as the last of his supplies were tap-dancing on the bottom of the basket he carried, he reached the far edge of town
and found himself before a vast field sown with crosses. With
all his accumulated happiness, he wrote "Cemetery," and sat
down to wait. Peacefully.

11. *Littleherb and the Infidels*

Afterward came the time when the Indians tried to save Littleherb. They succeeded only in prolonging his life a bit, a few
years at most, not much reckoned against the mountains.

Littleherb did not thank them, letting resignation lick the
wounds of his soul. (Stupid Indians. Completely accultur-
ated, having forgotten the secrets of their race, not knowing

what constitutes the final self-realization, the ultimate, most profound surrender.)

They had been watching him from above, and only deigned to go down to him when they saw him fall after two days of standing guard at the old cemetery. Up to then, he had remained erect, casting shade like a tree. They went to rescue him even though they did not approve of his way of disturbing the peace of Deadtown—little signs all over the place! For what? Signs they couldn't read, but which nonetheless restored its proper name to each building, putting each in its place. Now nobody would forget. They, at least, would not forget, and to better remember—to better recount it all to coming generations—they descended a second time to Deadtown to bear the man to the heights, to those windy plateaus where their grandparents had settled.

The stranger was brought up unconscious, not much of a burden to carry up the craggy slope. It was like rescuing a stray sheep, a lost animal, and returning it to the heights.

When he first opened his eyes, Littleherb saw an eagle fly by and said to himself: "I'm dead. If there's something alive, it must mean I'm dead, because in this town there is absolutely nothing."

When he heard voices, he hadn't the slightest doubt, and when he was asked, "What is your name?" he replied, "Littleherb," since that was how he wanted to figure in the register of souls.

The name Littleherb sounded familiar to the Indians, and they decided this fellow with the kind eyes must be one of them, in spite of his beard. They gave him something to eat— an activity Littleherb had almost forgotten—and bathed him, more to get the stink of Deadtown off him than to clean him up.

After this, they took him to the shrine of Fewfleas, and Littleherb had no choice but to fall in love with the young shaman.

· *Open Door*

She was like that: she had dazzling eyes. Dozens of lynx eyes, cleverly preserved, were arranged in an arc over her altar. The eyes formed a halo around Fewfleas, and Littleherb couldn't help but love her for her eyes.

When he was a bit fatter and somewhat recuperated, they were married most intimately, blessed by the winds.

The tenderness of Littleherb—who had achieved happiness and now needed nothing more—made Fewfleas forget some of her divinity and transformed her into the best of wives, two facts that cost her many subjects.

Within Littleherb, meanwhile, guilt began to blossom, growing and growing there high in the mountains till it reached the point that guilt almost sent him tumbling down the slope, back to Deadtown.

He took to spending long hours on the lip of the chasm, looking toward where Deadtown, Redtown, *His*town stood. But it was impossible, at that distance, to make it out. Because of its color and materials, it vanished into the landscape. Finally, as his own eyes were insufficient, he brought out to the cliff's edge the arc of lynx eyes from the altar of Fewfleas.

At night, the eyes served as tiny reflectors, and it was as if the invisible town was lit by thousands of fireflies. So Littleherb could locate exactly where he had christened every house.

Fewfleas, good wife to the end, came to fetch him when it got too late, and for a while would stand in wonder at the fireflies of the town. But only for a while. It seemed unwise to openly applaud other people's miracles.

Fewfleas wasn't the only one to wonder at the tiny, green lights that the lynx eyes seemed to project over Deadtown. Little by little, the whole tribe knew about the miracle and ended up clumped around Littleherb on the edge of the mountain.

Sometimes they had to forcefully restrain Littleherb, who wanted to launch himself head over heels to return to that peaceful felicity he had known in his adobe town. But more than the hands of the Indians, the voice of Fewfleas held him there, when she called him from their hut at that hour of a different joy, a moveable one.

While restraining Littleherb, the tribe embraced him, and finally came to worship him. That was the way Littleherb was: he awakened passions without wanting to, like the hatred of those people who had thrown stones at him.

Passions come and go. As it turned out, the Indians up above came to adore him as a god from the regions of light. And he himself began to believe that his ascension had not been in vain and that, in some yet unknowable way, he ought to return to the infidels what they had forgotten down in Redtown.

III. *The Second Founding of Redtown*

The Indians eventually took Littleherb for an oracle. Fewfleas dictated the words in his ear, and all he had to do was repeat them with great feeling, appending to each prophecy: "Happiness lies below in Redtown, Belletown, Towntown."

Fewfleas pinched him subtly to make him shut up, afraid the others might discover the subterfuge, now that the only thing her husband wanted, sickened by the highland winds, was to descend. But everyone looked upon him goggle-eyed, and thanks to the lights of Deadtown, they were even inclined to believe his words. He did work, it must be admitted, a certain number of miraculous cures by the laying on of hands, and he gave good counsel to the confused. In the end, one fine day, the Indians decided to undertake the journey down, bearing him along in a litter crowned with the halo of lynx eyes. First went the goats, as if opening up the road, then the pigs and the first men, single file, carrying cages of chickens. Admittedly, there was wisdom in all this: the animals knew how to choose the best path. It was not an easy descent. Surely not, hanging from the

· *Open Door*

rocks! But still they went, singing and playing the flute from stone to stone, sometimes slipping right to the edge of the abyss.

They arrived at the end of an exhausting day's travel. After looking around a bit, they understood the mystery of the celebrated fireflies—nothing more than the sparkling, on moonlit nights, of the phosphorescent paint Littleherb had happened to use to make the signs. But the Indians chose not to investigate further, to leave things as they were.

They did, however, worship the rock on the outskirts of town. There, boldly writ, was what they intuited to be Littleherb's secret name. In a gesture of real affection, he took a piece of coal and added, "And Fewfleas," and drew a heart with an arrow, which the Indians interpreted as a sign of good omen. They entered the town singing so loudly that the adobe walls began to tremble. Finally, on one particularly high note, the walls tumbled down thunderously in an ugly cloud of dust.

At first panic reigned, but then the collapse gave rise to considerable mirth. Littleherb was the only one who failed to see much comedy in it: his poor town reduced to rubble. And when the children began to play war with shards of adobe, he feared getting a piece in the face as in other, unfortunate times. But no, there were no attacks here where everyone adored him, and after a while, he decided to see the positive side of the disaster: that no-place town had been his alone; the new town they would build would be of stone, more resilient.

They chose the most appropriate color of stone for each house—red for the distinguished, pinkest for those of pleasure. The house of Littleherb and Fewfleas was nearly crimson and Fewfleas began to recover her various dignities, even the arc of eyes. Littleherb ceded them to her with no regrets, as she had once ceded them to him. And he found much more to his liking the role of living god than that of miracle worker.

He took to sitting in the afternoons on the rock inscribed

with his old name. Gazing west, he could recapture bits of that happiness he had known before.

He still played—perfectly, constantly—the part of a god, so deeply had he imbibed the idea. It wasn't for nothing that he had been born, suffered, and thought, and had come to the point of giving up there by the cemetery. He never returned there, and didn't much want to. His rock was enough. And he really did seem a god, sitting on that stone cross-legged, a soft wind or the cry of a bird rustling his beard. He had such wise eyes. He knew so many things, though he never spoke them.

A select member of the tribe had the honor of handing him his maté, made with aromatic herbs. Sometimes the sipper clogged, and as he sipped it made little noises that everyone marveled at. But the greatest marvel occurred the day he decided to teach them all to read, and at last they could decipher the meaning of those signs they revered as relics.

Veneration reached its peak when the entire tribe finally read effortlessly. That was indeed a glorious day for everyone, except for Littleherb. From then on, he had to write ever more complicated texts. The Indians loudly demanded new reading material, and complained bitterly when it wasn't to their liking. For more than a year, Littleherb wrote tirelessly while the others went about their simple labors—tilling the earth, tending the animals, or bartering with distant tribes.

Poor Littleherb! He didn't even have time to watch the rebirth of his old Deadtown, his beloved Redtown, so tightly did writing hem him in. Till the day arrived when he had written for the Indians their entire history and that of their town and, feeling himself fulfilled, he resigned from his task.

He forever renounced being a living god and lapsed into the comfortable role of priest-consort. It's the kind of life we all envy now, as we spend our days writing him stories. Like this one.

tr. Christopher Leland

· Open Door

Up
Among
the
Eagles

You'll find what I tell you hard to believe, for who knows anything, nowadays, about life in the country? And life here on the
mountains, up among the eagles. You get used to it. Oh yes, I
can tell you. I who never knew anything but the city, just look
at me now, the color of clay, carrying my pails of water from
the public fountain. Water for myself and water for others. I've
been doing it to eke out a living ever since the day I made the
foolish mistake of climbing the path that borders the cliff. I
climbed up and, looking down at the green dot of the valley
down below, I decided to stay here forever. It wasn't that I was
afraid, I was just being prudent, as they say: threatening cliffs,
beyond imagination—impossible even to consider returning.
Everything I owned I traded for food: my shoes, my wrist-
watch, my key holder with all the keys (I wouldn't be needing
them anymore), a ballpoint pen that was almost out of ink.

The only thing of any value I kept is my polaroid camera, no
one wanted it. Up here they don't believe in preserving im-

ages, just the opposite: every day they strive to create new images only for the moment. Often they get together to tell each other about the improbable images they've been envisioning. They sit in a circle in the dark on the dirt floor of their communal hut and concentrate on making the vision appear. One day, out of nothing, they materialized a tapestry of non-existent colors and ineffable design, but they decided that it was just a pale reflection of their mental image, and so they broke the circle to return the tapestry to the nothingness from which it had come.

They are strange creatures; normally they speak a language whose meaning they themselves have forgotten. They communicate by interpreting pauses, intonations, facial expressions, and sighs. I tried to learn this language of silences, but it seems I don't have the right accent. At any rate, they speak our language when they refer to trivial matters, the daily needs that have nothing to do with their images. Even so, some words are missing from their vocabulary. For example, they have no word for yesterday or for tomorrow, before or after, or for one of these days. Here everything is now, and always. An unsatisfactory imitation of eternity like the tapestry I have already mentioned. Have mentioned? Oh yes, I'm the only one to use that verb tense; I may also be the only one who has any notion of conjugation. A vice left over from the world down there, knowledge I can't barter because no one wants it.

Will you trade me some beans for a notion of time, I went around asking the women in the marketplace, but they shook their heads emphatically. (A notion of time? They looked at me with mistrust. A way of moving on a different plane? That has nothing to do with the knowledge they are after.)

Who dares speak of the passage of time to the inhabitants of this high place where everything endures? Even their bodies endure. Death neither decays nor obliterates them, it merely

· *Open Door*

stops them in their path. Then the others, with exquisite delicacy—a delicacy I've only seen them employ in connection with newly dropped kids or with certain mushrooms—carry the corpse beyond the rushing stream and with precise symmetry arrange it in the exact place it occupied in life. With infinite patience they have succeeded in creating, on the other side, a second town that obliterates time, an unmoving reflection of themselves that gives them a feeling of security because it is mummified, unmodifiable.

They only allow themselves changes in respect to the images. They grow, yes, they grow up and reach adulthood with only a suspicion of old age, remaining more or less the same until they die. In contrast, I discover with horror that I have a sprinkling of gray hairs, and wrinkles are lining my face; premature, of course, but who could keep her youth in this dry air, beneath such intense skies? What will become of me when they discover that time passes in my life, and is leaving its marks?

They are absorbed in other concerns, in trying to retain visions of what appear to be jewelled palaces and splendors unknown on this earth. They roam around latitudes of awe while all I can do—and very infrequently and with extreme stealth at that—is take a photo of myself. I am down to earth despite living in this elevated land floating among clouds. And they say the altitude deranges those of us who come from sea level. But it is my belief, my fear, that they are the ones who are deranged; it's something ancestral, inexplicable, especially when they are squatting on their haunches, as they almost always are, looking inward in contemplation. I'm always looking outward, I search every road, almost nonchalantly nourishing my fear. They watch me go by carrying water, the pole across my shoulders and the two pails dangling from it, and I would like to think they do not suspect my fear. This fear has two faces, not at all like the one that kept me from returning after I had climbed the mountain. No, this is not a simple fear; it reflects others, and becomes voracious.

On the other hand, I am here, now. That now grows and changes and expands with time and, if I am lucky, will continue to evolve. I do not want them to be aware of this evolving, as I have already said, and even less do I want to be like them, exempt from time. For what would become of me if I kept this face forever, as if surprised between two ages? I think about the mummies in the mirror city, oh yes, absolutely, only mummies are unchanged by time. Time does not pass for the dead, I told myself one day, and on a different day (because I, if not they, am very careful to relate question to calendar) I added: nor does it pass for those who have no concept of death. Death is a milestone.

The inhabitants here, with their language of silence, could teach me the secrets of the immobility that so closely resembles immortality, but I am not eager to learn them. Life is a movement toward death; to remain static is to be already dead.

Sit here, little lady, nice and quiet here with us is one of the few things they consent to say to me in my own language, and I shake my head energetically (one more way of insuring movement), and as soon as I am out of their sight, I begin to run like crazy along the neglected paths. More often than not I run up, not down, but either way, I don't want to get too far from the town, I don't want to stumble into the still city and find myself face-to-face with the mummies.

The secret city. I don't know its exact location but I know everything about it—or maybe I only suspect. I know it has to be identical to this humble little clump of huts where we live, a faithful replica with the exact same number of bodies, for when one of them dies the oldest mummy is thrown into the void. It's noisy in the secret city. The noise announces its proximity, but it also serves a more basic purpose: scraps of tin, of

· Open Door

every size and shape, hang from the rafters of the huts to scare away the buzzards. They are all that moves in the secret city, those scraps of tin to scare away the vultures, the only thing that moves or makes a sound. On certain limpid nights the wind carries the sound to where the living dwell, and on those nights they gather in the plaza, and dance.

They dance, but oh so slowly, almost without moving their feet, more as if they were undulating, submerged in the dense waters of sound. This happens only rarely, and when it does I feel an almost uncontrollable urge to join in the dance—the need to dance soaks into my bones, sways me—but I resist with all my strength. I am afraid that nothing could be more paralyzing than to yield to this music that comes from death. So that I won't be paralyzed I don't dance. I don't dance and I don't share the visions.

I have not witnessed a birth since I have been here. I know they couple, but they don't reproduce. They do nothing to avoid it, simply the stillness of the air prevents it. As for me, at this point I don't even go near men. It must be admitted that men don't come near me either, and there must be a reason, considering how often and how closely they approach almost anything else. Something in my expression must drive them away, but I've no way of knowing what it is. There are no mirrors here. No reflections. Water is either glaucous or torrential white. I despair. And every so often in the privacy of my cave, sparingly and with extreme caution, I take a new photo of myself.

I do this when I can't stand things any longer, when I have an overwhelming need to know about myself, and then no fear, no caution, can hold me back. One problem is that I am running out of film. In addition, I know perfectly well that if they find my photographs, if they place them in chronological order, two things can happen: they will either abominate or adore me. And neither possibility is to be desired. There are no alternatives. If they put the photos in order and draw the conclusions. If they see that when I arrived, my face was smoother, my hair brighter, my bearing more alert. If they discover the marks of time they will know that I have not controlled time even for a moment. And so if they find I am growing older, they won't want me among them, and they will stone me out of town, and I will have to face the terrifying cliffs.

I don't even want to think about the other possibility. That they will adore me because I have so efficiently, and so concretely, materialized these images of myself. Then I would be like stone to them, like a statue forever captive and contained.

Either of these two lapidary prospects should provide sufficient reason to restrain my suicidal impulse to take yet another photograph, but it doesn't. Each time, I succumb, hoping against hope that they will not be alerted by the glare of the flash. Sometimes I choose stormy nights; perhaps I conjure up the lightning with my pale simulacrum. At other times I seek the protective radiance of dawn, which at this altitude can be incendiary.

Elaborate preparations for each of my secret snapshots, preparations charged with hope and danger. That is, with life. The resulting picture does not always please me but the emotion of seeing myself—no matter how horrible or haggard I appear—is immeasurable. This is I, changing in a static world that imitates death. And I feel safe. Then I am able to stop and speak of simple things with the women in the market and even understand their silences, and answer them. I can live a little longer without love, without anyone's touch.

Until another relapse, a new photo. And this will be the last. On a day with the sound of death, when the minimal activities of the town have come to a halt and they have all congregated to dance in the marketplace. That deliberate dancing that is like praying with their feet, a quiet prayer. They will never admit it, but I suspect that they count to themselves, that their

· *Open Door*

dance is an intricate web of steps like knitting, one up, two backward, one to the right. All to the tinkling of the far-off tin scraps: the wind in the house of the dead. A day like any other; a very special day for them because of the sound that they would call music, were they interested in making such distinctions. But all that interests them is the dance, or believing they are dancing, or thinking of the dance, which is the same thing. To the pulse of the sound that floods over us, whose origins I cannot locate though I know it comes from the city of the dead.

They do not call to me, they don't even see me. It's as if I didn't exist. Maybe they're right, maybe I don't exist, maybe I am my own invention, or a peculiar materialization of an image they have evoked. That sound is joyful, and yet the most mournful ever heard. I seem to be alive, and yet . . .

I hide in my cave trying not to think, trying not to hear the tinkling; I don't know where it comes from, but I fear where it may lead me. With the hope of setting these fears to rest, I begin my preparations for the last photo: a desperate attempt to recover my being. To return to myself, which is all I have.

Anxiously, I wait for the perfect moment, while outside, darkness is weaving its blackest threads. Suddenly, an unexpected radiance causes me to trip the shutter before I am ready. No photograph emerges, only a dark rectangle that gradually reveals the blurred image of a stone wall. And that's all. I have no more film so I may as well throw away the camera. A cause for weeping were it not for the fact the radiance is not fading. A cause for uneasiness, then, because when I peer out I see that the blazing light is originating from the very place I wanted not to know about, from the very heart of the sound, from a peak just below us. And the radiance comes from millions of glittering scraps of tin in the moonlight. The city of the dead.

Spontaneously, I set forth with all my stupid photos, responding to an impulse that responds, perhaps, to a summons from the sonorous radiance. They are calling me from down there, over to the left, and I answer, and at first I run along the treacherous path and when the path ends I continue on. I stumble, I climb and descend, I trip and hurt myself; to avoid hurtling into the ravine I try to imitate the goats, leaping across the rocks; I lose my footing, I slip and slide, I try to check my fall, thorns rake my skin and at the same time hold me back. Rashly I pull ahead and it is imperative I must reach the city of the dead and leave my face to the mummies. I will place my successive faces on the mummies and then at last I'll be free to go down without fearing stone for I'll take my last photo with me and I am myself in that photo and I am stone.

tr. Margaret Sayers Peden

The Attainment

of Knowledge

The senses and gods intersect in these parts of the world, assuming these parts are of the world and not strung over the Andes, just beyond arm's reach. Above, an anguished blue. If only they knew, if they knew of that anguish. But no. They recognize neither the desolation nor the blue. So many centuries living on their false islands made of straw, floating on the lake, islands regenerated daily; so many generations come and gone, nearly walking on water over these islands of rushes. Almost like Christ if they only knew. But they don't even know that, as they sail their rafts that are extensions of those islands—just as yellow, just as bright.

They know, yes, about the absence of sound, because their ears have been blessed so as to catch silence's most subtle nuances. That is why I say that the gods and senses intermingle in these latitudes. I also say it because, for them, the most sublime of states is color-blindness. A pure achromatope is venerated for the gift of standing undazzled before that inhuman blue that is the blue of the lake, before its reflection in the sky, before the sun's beating on the golden straw. Too much chromatic intensity for so much silence—that is why those who can perceive no color at all enjoy at least the dignity of priests.

More than one among them has claimed to see in black and white, feigning confusion, even mistaking the line of the horizon, but the imposture does not disturb anyone there on the lid of the world. He who sees no colors is only greatly blessed within himself. The meager propitiations that on occasion his fellows render up are of little use.

Thus life goes by—briefly. Few of these people live to fifty. The old ones are more beloved than condemned, but they maintain a minimum of contact with the rest of the tribe.

They have lasted, growing wise, and for that very reason nobody wants to listen to them. Everyone dreams of building an enormous glass cage, so they might be seen but not heard. However, there is no way to get glass in the highlands. They encountered glass here only once, and that would have been fatal had they not lived on the water. The little piece of glass was lovely and much admired until it so focused the sun's rays that a fire started. It was the first fire in their history, and nearly the last. It flared on a newly constructed island and the fresh straw burned for a long time, till the island burned its way free of the tangle of reeds and began to drift. A fire ship.

On the island was a hut of rushes and an old woman of material indistinguishable from that of which mortals are made.

They floated away—those flames that had once been an island with its old woman and her hut—and from a distance provided such a spectacle that, for the first time, the common folk rejoiced in their ability to see colors, because red had not been part of their known spectrum up to that time. (The honored color-blind missed the flames, to their eventual misfortune: they did not know the color of combustion.)

The old woman of the island, on the other hand, knew

· *Open Door*

more: she found out about heat and even the horror of burns. She learned too how the fire swallowed her cries, and when finally the water vanquished the flames, she remained floating on that immensity of the lake—that sea on the tip of the earth—on a tiny, charred island. She began to notice that her knowledge had grown with the heat of the flames, and she felt infinitely wiser than before, having survived her forced pilgrimage. But wise for what? To be unable to transmit it to anyone, as usual, especially among those who know only the ineffable (the wisdom of those on their floating islands of fresh straw, and that of us all who believe ourselves secure with our feet firmly on the ground).

But the old woman wanted to break the vote of silence, and so, in the middle of that lake so blue it seemed dreamt, impossible, indigo, she decided to communicate to the others what she had come to know. She decided to make them learn, at least, the lesson of fire. If she could only send them a spark! But no spark could brave the diaphanous air nor sail over the water. A defenseless spark, tiny button of light. And anyway, her island had, by now, cooled off. Not even the sweet warmth of embers remained.

From fire to flame, from flame to ember to warm ash, to that other ash, dry and sterile, that with the wind's help covers everything with gray. These had been luminous transformations—pure, internal joy in no way comparable to simple happiness.

To tell them about the heat beyond that of the sun. She wanted to share the wisdom of fire with the others, with her brothers, those who, though beneath the sun, are unaware of any kind of warmth.

The old, gray woman, covered with soot, a bit charred, poor old thing, scorched in places and, beneath that gray dusting of ash, completely browned not so much from the sun as by master fire, which had instilled in her own flesh the principle of cooking. And that, among so much other good news, was what she wanted to communicate to her fellows: the possibility of transforming oneself at the same time the flame transforms the matter. Such is the alchemical power of that inconceivable red and burning being that she did not even know was called fire.

She searched for signs of life, plunging her hands into the ashes, sinking her forearms up to the elbows, knowing that the danger of getting burned was, for her, no danger at all. And after much searching she found a tiny glow beating in the heart of the ash. With that minuscule firebrand and the charcoal that had formed, she kept for months the humble blaze alive. It didn't even occur to her to cook her dried fish over it, not wishing to defile it. And she tenderly went about remaking her island. Harvesting new rushes that grew in the lake, she put them to dry in the sun and covered, bit by bit, that bed of ashes with the buoyant reeds. Afterwards, she rebuilt her hut with the same rushes.

When she felt complete, she set it all afire, thinking that somehow the others would understand her message, thanks to the dark cloud the flames would send aloft. In this way, without meaning to, she reinvented smoke signals. It was as useless as reinventing the telegraph. In sum, another worthless holocaust: the others far off could not or would not decipher her message.

Perhaps they already knew.

tr. Christopher Leland

· *Open Door*

One Siren

or Another

"Now you tell me it's a dream. But if you really meddled in this dream of mine, if you dared to cut in like that, then you're mine too, because you are part of my dream."

Bullshit! the captain wanted to shout. What rubbish you're spouting. You're crazy.

Still, because he's in the man's hands and feels sorry for him:

"A sailor's life is hard enough. There was no need for you to do this to us."

"Mine's harder, and nobody does anything to or for me. Neither good nor bad. Nobody cares about me. Only you with your damned ship, butting into my continent and cutting it in half and surely killing people, my people, and now you're cool as a cucumber."

"Cool! No. Desperate. When the boat ran up on the sand, the propeller was seriously damaged. A death rattle all through the ship like we'd collided with a whale and it was just the damned sandbanks of your little atoll. We've busted a blade of the propeller, I think, and it's all your fault, because for some crazy reason you turned out the damned light on the lighthouse in the middle of the night. And so we run aground. You failed in your duty. You've committed a crime. Your duty was to warn us off the reefs, not to attract us like flypaper."

"Duty. Look who's talking. You're the captain of the ship and a ship ought to sail on water, not come butting up on land and sinking continents even if they're only dreams."

"All right. Enough, I've had it with these stories. Please. I told you, there was nobody there. Just water. A smooth sheet of water, the same clear water as anywhere else except that it was nighttime, so the same black water, calm as you please."

"You didn't hear the music?"

"How was I going to hear music?"

"And you didn't see them dancing?"

"I didn't see them, did not see them. I saw nothing. And I was on the bridge all night, at the second officer's side, because it was hot and because we had wandered a little off course. Nothing more than that. But I would have seen them. There was this glow."

"At least you admit that: you saw the shimmering. That's the halo that surrounds my continent."

"Okay. Enough. I'm going to sleep. I'm going back to the ship to wait for the high tide. I think we can float free with no problem, then I'll see about the propeller. I'll send some divers down; if necessary we can cut the opposite blade so at least the screw's balanced."

"You're not going anywhere. You're staying here with me to shoot the breeze. Now that you liquidated my people, the least you can do is provide a little conversation."

"I didn't liquidate anybody. I'm going to my boat."

"Go ahead. But I took the precaution of slipping the lines on it. It should have drifted a good ways by now."

· *Open Door*

"I'm going to signal the crew to come and get me the best way they can. They can rig up a raft if need be."

"I don't see how you're going to signal them. I've got the flares and I don't intend to give them to you even if you kill me. You also know that I'm armed."

"Why should I care if you're armed? I'm not threatening you. You've got no reason to threaten me. Right now, all I want to do is go to sleep and forget about the ship. I don't see how that could bother you."

"I only wish I could forget about the ship too, the damned ship. It slammed through the middle of my continent like there was a canal there. Slammed through big as you please, puffed up with all its lights. I'm sure my people would have applauded from the bank, if there had been a canal. But there wasn't. It split the land in half, cut it like a knife—the knife of the prow—and brought on the flood. Now it's a sunken continent. Come out here on the pier, just take a look. Now you can't see anything."

"And what was I supposed to see?"

"Don't be so skeptical. I told you. You could see infinite lights in the night. It was beautiful. With a telescope, you could even make out figures singing and dancing. They were always celebrating at night. Surely they were celebrating the mere fact of being alive."

"They were only alive in your imagination. Forget them. Tomorrow is another day."

"So what. I know it's another day and days don't mean a thing to me. They're empty and most of the time I sleep. The sun makes me sleep. Only twilight interests me, when the time comes to light the lighthouse. I've got something like a light meter inside me that wakes me when the sun is low. But tomorrow too there'll be another night and at night I can't sleep. I have to be alert. And they helped me and gave me strength. When the wind blew from that direction it carried their music and it was always a music of hope. I thought I'd join them after I retired. Or died. It's the same thing. They were waiting for me, and now nobody is waiting for me."

"We can wait for you, if you want, when we make port."

"For all the good that would do me. You're just like anybody else. They were different."

"How do you know? We're different, too. We've sailed a good deal and we can tell you lots of stories."

"What good are your stories to me? I can give you a brand new one and not even brag about it. We could call it the mad watchman who thought he could see Atlantis (we'll call it so as not to complicate things). Because really you can't call it Atlantis here in the south. It was a secret continent and you cut it in two like a thread cuts butter. Shit."

"Go ahead. Go ahead. Get it all out."

"Yeah, go on, be magnanimous. I get it all out and you feel real generous and think you've soothed a madman. Only, generous or not, you won't be able to give me my continent back, and now, what do I do nights? How am I going to pass the time without them? What sense does my life make now?"

"One of these days, your life may make real sense. You're the lighthouse keeper, captain of the lighthouse, think about it."

"It's pure professional deformation."

"That's not why I said it; I said it because I meant it. Where did you learn to talk that way anyway?"

"I read sometimes, you know."

"All right. Read some more, to take your mind off things. Or read less. Some things can really turn you around. Look at Don Quixote."

"Some things? And you, what turned you around? I ask because this life of wandering around the South Atlantic—none too hospitable—what kind of life is that? You can't be quite in your right mind. The water is a monster. It's the soft skin of a monster hiding beasts we've never even dreamed of. A skin that looks glossy, seething with horrors underneath. At least I see it from the relative safety of a coast, but you and your friends float over that skin that bristles up and then you're at its mercy. I don't envy you."

"Well, turnabout is fair play. I don't envy you stranded forever on this godforsaken island."

"I wouldn't say forever. I had other plans . . . And as for 'stranded,' it has a certain rootedness to it. You, on the other hand, just drift."

"What do you mean, drift? We know exactly where we're going even if now and then we get a few degrees off course, to your inconvenience and our misfortune. But that's really insignificant. The important thing is that we move. We go from one place to another. We have a goal that spurs us on and bears us to safe harbor. Back there, we find women and booze and listen to that music you thought you heard in the distance. In port, we feel it all the way down to our bones. Let me go over to the ship for a couple bottles at least. That way, we can talk better about our wanderings."

"You're not going anywhere. If you want music, sing. I'm not going to stop you, but I won't insist either. It's rare I have the chance to talk to somebody. The people who bring the provisions and gas cylinders for the light only come every couple months, and then only when they can bring the ship to shore, because the storms that hit in these parts are unforgiving. And even so, they're not a very talkative bunch; they're really pretty brusque. They come when they can, they leave me what I need, and they go with hardly a word. And to top it all off, they'll be late in coming this time because it's storm season. The sea can get rough from one minute to the next, in which case they don't like to even get close. There are a lot of rocks around the light. But don't worry. We've got enough provisions and we can stay here for months without going hungry."

"And my crew? There are eleven men on that ship waiting for me. Maybe we can float free with the tide."

"Don't even think about it. If the sea pulls you off the sand, it will throw you against the rocks. Where you're aground, the tide is weak. You can only wait for the storm, and the storm's merciless. Now the lightning's started, see? It won't be long before the storm breaks. The barometer's very low."

"The wireless man should have radioed the shore by now. They'll be here soon to rescue us."

"Soon? Do you know how far we are from dry land? They'll be a long time coming. Too long. If I were you, I'd forget about it. Have some more tea. There are bagsful down in the cellar."

"Enough jokes. When they come, they'll arrest you if I tell them what happened. But if you let me go now, then I'll forget the whole thing and I won't press charges against you for having cut the light at the crucial moment. You made us run aground, and we might have broken up on the rocks. You're guilty of a serious crime."

"And who'll believe you? Your word against mine, Captain, and I've had this job for almost forty years with an excellent record. Why on earth would I put out the light? And a momentary lapse wouldn't cut off the gas accidentally . . . You're a young man, Captain, and your crew may not survive to testify in your behalf. It was your mistake, Captain. What were you doing in these waters? I'm not the one who went off course. But I'm not planning to accuse you, Captain, unless you force me to. Think about it."

"Shut up, for God's sake! My men are calling me. Can't you hear the siren?"

"Siren? What siren? You're raving, Captain. The only sirens were the ones on my little continent and you forced them away forever. How can you expect me to hear those others that don't even sing?"

tr. Christopher Leland

· *Open Door*

The Blue

Water

Man

They pointed him out to me: He's the water man they said, and I drew closer to him because I liked the word, not because of the importance the title implies in these parts, the right to distribute the rationed water as he pleases. But it wasn't me who lit the wick. Even though I got pretty close, like some people say, and got to touch him (there are witnesses for everything— there's someone unscrupulous enough to tell the truth: imagination is withering and nothing is left for the poor.

It seems I did get to touch him—water man and all—so the witnesses say. But it wasn't me who lit the wick, I swear. The idea of the explosion didn't even occur to me.

Water man. Someone respectable in appearance, someone worthy of living in this town so full of respect for the fallen leaf, for the hungry dog, for what's already dying and for who's patiently awaiting the end: the human being.

(The cemetery has tombs in bright colors. The houses in this part of the world are adobe. While we're on this earth it's best we blend in with it.)

The water man, on the other hand, was the only one dustless in the village—something almost insulting.

Stone, dust and stone, all the streets wind toward that wide strain of light: the marketplace. Up there, the water man shimmers, clean in his white shirt and gold teeth and his moustache. Below, we walk carting buckets of water from the river already running dry.

That happened on Sunday and a week has gone by.

I did not light the wick, nor did I have anything to do with the explosion.

He was clean down to his toes in the courtyard of the old convent, and I was filthy as ever, covered with dust. Still fresh on my fingertips was the indigo I had been painting the walls with (my house is adobe like all the others and I was slowly painting it to soften it: I wanted a touch of blue to make it seem like water). (And if some witness says I touched him, well, maybe I did touch him, though I think it was his hands over my body and not the inadmissable opposite.)

It was Palm Sunday, to be exact, and he was in the courtyard calculating profits. He was a vile water man without a doubt: for a hundred pesos, he would let the cisterns of the rich overflow, while their neighbors could get struck by lightning for all he cared. He was the spider in the middle of a web of plumbing, god of an underground world of sewers.

(And to think that by only moving a finger, by shaking off the mantle of greed and generously opening the spillways, he could have quenched the thirst of the whole town.)

· *Open Door*

On his chest, a blue stain remained that Sunday—Palm Sunday—almost hidden beneath his white shirt. That was all.

And a week went by:

Monday—I took him ten pesos I'd hoarded (never mind how) and so got a trickle of water from my spigot, enough to keep my three turkeys and the neighbor's pig from dying of thirst.

Tuesday—The tourists had left and I couldn't get another peso. But thanks to human nature (weak, weak, weak!), I got him to let that trickle continue. I washed my underwear.

Wednesday—I continued painting my house blue in absolute silence. As the afternoon waned, I went to see him for a while. Both the water man's arms, his chest, and part of his back were blue.

Maundy Thursday—We were in the courtyard, waiting in vain for the reenactment of the Last Supper. Isn't there even enough water for this humble pageant? That thought wasn't mine, it came from someone who dismounted in front of the gate and said: "Even if it is the last one, after supper the dishes have to be washed. With what water? No show tonight, my friends. You can go on home."

Good Friday—We walked the Way of the Cross today, logically enough, with the procession and prayers and parched lips and cracked skin. (The rich stroll by, the ones from the hilltop houses, exchanging discreet smiles with the water man. His pockets are bulging and the rich have their swimming pools full, all the water they want. As for us, we don't have even a drop left for tears.)

Holy Saturday—Quiet all through the town, and in my life as well. Only the water man's left hand, his face, and one testicle remain flesh-colored. The rest of him is indigo. I wonder how. Only the children are out today, and the dogs like drying hides staked on four legs.

From my window, I saw the truck arrive with the Judases—red devils with horns—and I confess I said to myself: Our Judas is blue, and we're truly afraid of him. He's not made of papier-mâché. He isn't hollow inside. He's evil to the core.

I also saw without paying much attention how they stuffed firecrackers in the stomach of each effigy, put a string of firecrackers around the neck and wound the wicks in between the horns (but it's one thing to see and another to think about how you might use what you see).

(Everybody saw it. After four hundred years, they all know more about it than I do, coming from so far away, even if I do feel close to them. I swear, it wasn't me. Don't make that old mistake: don't single out the stranger, even with a blessing.)

(The color of your house, they told me later, and I shrugged my shoulders: the color of *his* tomb.)

And at eleven at night they called us to mass with wooden rattles.

Easter Sunday—At midnight: wild bell-ringing. As if the town still had so much spirit. At one, there was a volley of fireworks, and at two-thirty, the first rains fell, putting an end to the long months of drought. What a welcome visitation! How long awaited! Finally, we didn't need him anymore . . . (It rained all night; it rained in the morning till mass at eleven and the people, there at the convent, gave thanks to heaven for the only thing heaven had to offer them. And they prayed on their knees, showing off feet soled with mud.)

· *Open Door*

At noon the sun reappeared, unaware of the bliss. And do you think, amid the suffocating whirls of steam I could have gathered the strength to conceive the idea? Between the hellish heat and the blasts of the firecrackers. In the marketplace, the papier-mâché Judases exploded in a million pieces. Evil itself went up in smoke and the people knew it and rejoiced.

At five in the afternoon, the fireworks intensified and the fiesta began. I ran to the marketplace to see the men of the town dancing around heaps of mangoes and bananas, watermelon stands and earthen cooking pots. Dazzling colors shimmered like leaves washed by the rain. I was just about to join in the festivities of the townspeople dressed up like lords: velvet tunics; huge, brightly embroidered hats; lace and tinsel; whiteman's masks with pointy beards; white gloves. I wanted to celebrate with them, join in the brassy music. I wanted to commune with the people, until I saw the water man, that son of a bitch.

He was standing on the fountain in the middle of the marketplace. I saw him from the back as his eyes searched the crowd (sought me, surely), now dressed in blue, complete. Blue atop the dry fountain—the water man. That was too much, and though my job wasn't finished—the left hand, the face, and one testicle—I couldn't help myself and fled in panic. As they noticed me, leaving at a run, the inexpressive faces of those masks with eyes (who ever heard of such a thing!) followed my escape. And he above, so indigo, irreverent.

With my last pesos, I bought white paint (home is more demanding than hunger. I didn't want a house the color of the water man. I wanted a pure house).

The Judases blew apart in the plaza and to the rhythm of the firecrackers I swung my arm in broad strokes and my house—

electric azure—began to fade, turning to a soft, transparent blue. I had whitewashed almost an entire wall when I heard an explosion like dynamite, like a giant skyrocket.

There was a tense beat of waiting—suspense in the air—and then, panting, they came to bring me the news.

He had been the great Judas, close to the real one. When I got to the marketplace, no one was dancing, and the masks surveyed the scene with their inhuman eyes. The water man was there gutted, impaled on the highest point of the fountain.

(A stick of dynamite stuck in his fly, or a fistful of cherry bombs in his navel.)

This for certain: it was not me who lit the wick, as you can surmise by reading my statements carefully.

His face—it was weird—his face was a soft, transparent blue, as was one hand turned palm up. I would swear too that one testicle had turned that same blue, but it was torn off when his guts blew up and they never found it. (The guts spattered slightly the people from the hilltop houses, who were close by, sitting at the only tables with tablecloths in the middle of the plaza, slowing down the dancing, sipping politely at their drinks, showing off their embroidered shirts or their long dresses. They only got spattered a little, but they stood up, thoroughly disgusted, and gathered up their dear little children to take them away from that ill-fated spectacle.)

I, on the other hand, stayed to await the miracle: from the blasted belly of this Judas water would forever flow.

The townspeople had lower expectations. From the blasted belly, blood flowed—not surprising anybody and to the delight of many. Those wearing masks dipped their white-gloved fingers in the blood and streaked the white, white-man's masks that covered their faces.

· *Open Door*

Blood of the water man, symbol of water, perfect ablution. Afterward, they wanted to bear me through the streets. They loved me and hated me and cried out my name. And I, as always so unworthy, so abandoned, while the blue water man turns red, and not even his color belongs to me any more.

tr. Christopher Leland

My

Everyday

Colt

I.

Today I fell off my horse. Lord knows, it happens more and more often, falling off my horse. I try everything: putting on perfume, plucking my eyebrows, smiling, and even acting a little silly, but it's no good: I fall off my horse. He's a stubborn animal, and testy. He bucks enough to throw me before I even try to mount him. An animal that can figure out my intentions, a psychic horse. I try to stroke his flank and he only bristles; he won't take sugar from my hand, nothing. Goddamned colt, more of a torture rack than a horse. Shitty animal.

Horse, you shit, I say to him, and he pricks up his ears but doesn't listen to me. He strikes poses like that, my horse, indifferent to anything that smacks of tenderness.

The bad thing about this whole business is the others: when another one of us turns into a horse and then won't let anybody mount him or even teach him how to eat out of your hand . . . I don't have hands anymore. The horses have nipped them off bit by bit, mistaking them for the pieces of sugar I give them

· *Open Door*

out of the goodness of my heart. This is what happens with a sugar shortage. They all get so jumpy and as soon as you produce the merest lump of the stuff the first one to get to you chomps down and obliterates whatever it's grabbed.

So that's how I lost my hands. It's not so serious, really, but it makes riding a little complicated because I can't hold the reins. It isn't that I ever really wanted to hold the reins, but I can't control my wild colt with just my knees or other movements of my body. My colt doesn't care for anything phony: he demands a strong hand and hands I don't have. I'd really like to control him with spittle. God help us, I want to control him with a look and it's he who controls me.

There is a horse for each of us. Mine is dappled, looks like he'd be gentle, and yet it's hard for me to count to ten and still stay on him. You faggot horse, I tell him, but he doesn't flinch because he knows he's a prime stud. Nobody has told him (at least, I've been very careful not to let him know), nor does he get much chance to compare himself with others, but he still suspects it in spite of certain failures. My colt is a real stud and the only reason I don't show him at the State Fair is for fear he'll become even more stuck on himself. He's not a humble colt, no way. He torments me plenty with his demands. He makes me go at a gallop; forces me to overcome incredible obstacles. And I, always, clenching his mane in my teeth so he doesn't get away from me, because we shouldn't let our horse escape no matter how much of a mustang he may be.

With his mane clenched in my teeth, I snap back and forth like a pennant in the wind while my colt plunges on full tilt. He passes as close as he can to trees to slam me against the trunks, but I hang in there, skinned and bleeding, with an air of indifference so he can't enjoy his triumph: a triumphant horse is no mount at all.

And I, firmly on his back, despite the fact that I'm really not happy about the whole business. It actually infuriates me, and

I slip out of the stirrups. My horse takes advantage of those moments, but I keep him under control with my thighs. I stick to him like a squid. I do it for his own good. I don't even like to think of how bad he'd feel if he succeeded in throwing me. That's why I end up ragging on him a little, because he'd feel so alone, and yet he fights so hard to get me off of him, to get away from me.

He must be pretty crazy, wanting to push me away from him, and I who know what that means do what I can to stay astride my colt, for his own good, because without me he wouldn't be a horse. He would be just one more of them, and in his prior human form he wouldn't be able to let go with those magnificent whinnies or gallop as fast as he likes or feel a mustang's freedom.

And to let him go back to what he was, just like that, that would be an uncalled-for turn of the screw, hard and tight, too much like betrayal for my taste. And that's the last thing I would want. I don't want him to feel I've dragged him out of the world of horses as he was once dragged by anonymous hands from the human one. Thrown out suddenly from what, up to that point, he thought was paradise.

And here's the story.

I I.

He was running down the street, not looking back. Why bother, no one was chasing him. He knew that perfectly well. What he didn't know was the real reason for these sudden urges to escape that struck him in the midst of an otherwise pleasant stroll. And this time, as always, nobody was on his heels, but up ahead, half a block maybe, he saw them coming, boldly drawn against the clear sky in their neat blue uniforms. He wanted to rein himself in, to turn around muttering to himself

· *Open Door*

as if nothing was happening, but it was too late. The pair of them grabbed him, one on each arm, and the cop whose right hand was free punched him on the left temple. The fingers holding his arms relaxed, allowing him to slip easily to the sidewalk. And the two policemen continued on with their elastic gait, the creases in their pants impeccable, and he remained like a rag there in a doorway. For a long time no one felt moved to come to his aid.

Then something occurred that is hard to explain: the door opened with a squeak and a pair of hands dragged him, with some difficulty, into the house. Something inside him tried to resist this assistance, something in him wanted to keep running, just running, but that was impossible, with his head feeling like it could explode and his legs refusing to support him.

He could do nothing but allow himself to be borne along in a fog, and for quite a while he could only let things happen: he was settled into bed, there were cold compresses, some strong whiskey pressed to his lips, an unknown person taking his pulse or holding his hand compassionately. Except that, except that . . . When he could finally open his eyes after a long battle with his own eyelids, horror rose suddenly from his gut to his mouth and he cried:

"I'm blind!"

"What do you mean blind, my friend. Don't be an alarmist. We've blindfolded you, that's all. So the light doesn't damage your eyes. But, why hide it, it's also so you don't suffer any more damage by seeing what you would see. So calm down and rest easy."

"Easy! Who are you? Why are you talking to me like that? Why so pretentious, damn it! I'm in some gay whorehouse, in a ministry, in a jail. If I see you, you'll make mincemeat out of me. If I don't see, I'll go crazy."

Once again, someone took his hand. It must be the same guy, he thought, and he tried to pull away disgustedly. "Now,

now." It was a woman's voice, excessively sweet. "Grrr," he growled, but left his hand where it was, giving it up to the stroking. Another hand fell upon him—one too large for his tastes, but how could he be sure of dimensions: unable to grope, his eyes covered. The other hand (Doesn't feel like a woman's to me, damn it!) caressed his and he felt like singing "I Wanna Hold Your Hand" or something like that to break the tension building inside him, but the sweet, sweet voice of the woman interrupted:

"Let us take care of you. Have faith in us. After all, we did snatch you out of the hands of the police."

(Stuck on those upper extremities, aren't they, he thought. Are they extremists? He began to panic, inclined to such easy associations because of that pounding ache in his temple.)

"Don't strain yourself trying to figure out who we are or other things like that," the man said to him. "It's not important to you. The important thing is that you heal quickly so we can get you out of here."

"Now!" he demanded. He tried to sit up and cried out and fell back again. A clawing pain tore down the back of his head: the echo of a well-placed blow.

"Fighting makes the man, but stubbornness will unmake you twice as fast. Stay quiet or it will go badly for you."

With all its connotations, "go badly" was too much for him and a few tears, half-ashamed, began to moisten his blindfold. And he was afraid. Afraid that, because of the tears, the blindfold might grow transparent, leaving him suddenly looking at, for example, beings without faces, or faces that no one should be permitted to gaze upon. He began to imagine all kinds of monsters, shapeless things that his reason rejected while darker parts of his brain delightedly remolded them. Then, the noise that had begun to slowly escape his lips grew involuntarily to a low moan. He, the compulsive runner, the born marathoner, now tossed on an anonymous bed, invisible, unable to move. He saw the two policemen advancing on him down

· *Open Door*

the street, appearing out of nowhere, out of the depths of this very house, from some dark corner of the garden. They came at him and their feet were the treads of tanks that would simply crush him and they crushed him.

"Now, now. Calm down a little. You'll be able to go soon. Don't be upset. Don't give up hope. Don't suffer."

Don't suffer. Like a command. Nice idea, especially for someone who cannot control the pain running out of his head and spilling with undiminished intensity all through his body.

Don't suffer, don't hear, don't look, don't think. Good joke. A good analogy to what the nation expects of him, if it weren't for those surges of unimaginable pain that shook him in waves. Rippling waves, he thought, an idiotic thought when one is so close to terror and knows it.

The soft, soft hand strokes him again and he can't move his own hands to return the caresses or even grope a little. Part of his horror comes from this: he does not want to or cannot figure out if his inability to move is intrinsic or extrinsic, if it is born of a brain battered to the point it cannot transmit orders to his body or if the blame lies with a strong rope binding him.

Preparing. All his life preparing for whatever contingency, and now this, not knowing where he is—flat on his back to boot—with a hand caressing him, a hand perhaps affectionate, or lustful, or one of refined cruelty.

Suddenly the voice murmurs something like *poor thing*, and the hand twines over his arm and loosens his tie and opens two or three buttons of his shirt, stroking his neck with abandon. Ought he to love this hand, lick it? Or should he bite it? He wavers between those two equally canine responses and knows in any case he can choose neither. He can't move, nor can he articulate a word, much less think. Then how is it he is thinking now? How is it that these images keep wandering around his head as if nothing were happening, ideas running around in circles, as directionless as when he ran through the streets of the city. City? What city? Where? At what point on the map of fear? Ideas galloping like the hands now over his body, hands like spiders. There are two, no, four, four hands exploring his thighs, his loins, his breasts, opening buttons, undressing him, and the pain descends in puffs from his skull, bathing him with cold, with anguish, with fear, with fury, with pleasure.

It's a good thing he can't see us, the voices say. He can hear us, the voices answer. You can hear us, baby, can't you. You're right here with us even if you're playing possum. It's not so easy running all over the world. All that running can be pretty dangerous.

"Why were you running, you fool?" they shout at him.

"Why are you always running when you ought to be walking, lead-footed, at a nice measured pace?"

A nag, he thinks, they want me to be a nag and I'm a racehorse.

Something like a laugh escapes his clenched lips and it sounds like a whinny.

"You animal!" they yell.

Of course, he thinks, naturally, he thinks, and he only thinks now because now he can't really say this mouth is mine, this face is mine.

Whose are these withers; whose, these flanks; whose, these hooves, this dense mane, these fetlocks? Whose are these ears? The hand that caresses him asks these questions as it molds him. Meanwhile, another hand or hands punish him. Whose is this croup? That other hand screams at him, slapping him, and he doesn't want—nor is he able—to stamp with impatience, rear up.

"You are a colt," they say to him. And he knows it isn't true, in this moment at least it is not yet true, in this first stage of a poor mustang about to be broken, at the point of losing everything and accepting the bit.

tr. Christopher Leland

· *Open Door*

Papito's
Story

A thin wall has always separated us. Now the time has come for
the wall to unite us.

I had never paid much attention to him in the elevator, nor
when we walked down the long hall leading to our respective
apartments. He was self-absorbed, lugging along with him all
the trivialities of the daily commute on the train—smoke that
steamed up the mirrors of the entry hall, shouted conversations that stuck in his ears and made him deaf to my polite chit-
chat: Pretty day, isn't it. Or more likely: Looks like rain. Or:
This elevator, it gets more rickety every day.

A few times, he answered—Yes, no, indiscriminately. And
I shuffled those monosyllables of his and put them where I
pleased. I guess I liked the freedom he gave me to organize our
little dialogues according to my own logic.

There are things about him I could not appreciate until tonight: his hunched shoulders, that gray face barely translu-
cent, his wrinkled suits, his waning youth. (Yet tonight I

should have put my hand through the wall and made him accept our bond once and for all.)

In the end, he was the one to blame for the uproar that woke me up. And I—Julio—thought they were banging and kicking on my door, and that Open-up-you-son-of-a-bitch was addressed to me. What did the police want with me, I asked myself half-asleep, searching all up and down my pajamas for a weapon.

We'll smash the door open, they shouted. Give up. We've got the whole block surrounded.

My door, unscathed. And I knew then that they were one apartment over, and that he, so blank, so forgettable, was now offering me his one moment of glory and rebellion.

I couldn't open my door to see the cops' faces, drugged with loathing. The loathing of those who believe they are right is one step beyond reason, and I'd rather not confront it.

So I remained there, and glued my ear to the wall to offer him my company, and I don't know if I was happy to discover that someone was with him already. The woman's voice had the sharp ring of hysteria:

"Give yourself up. What's going to happen to me? Give up."

And he, so forgettable up to now, now gaining stature:

"No. I won't give up."

"Yes. Give yourself up. They'll knock the door down and kill me. They'll kill us both."

"Fuck them. We'll kill ourselves first. Come on. Kill yourself with me."

"You're crazy, Papito. Don't say that. I was good to you. Be good to me now, Papito."

I start to cough, my apartment is filling with tear gas. I run to open a window, though I would like to stay with my ear pressed to the wall—stay with you, Papito.

I open the window. It's true, you're surrounded, Papito.

· *Open Door*

Loads of police and an assault vehicle. All for you, and you so alone.

"There's a woman with me. Let her go," Papito shouts, "let her go or I'll shoot. I'm armed."

Bang! shouts the revolver to prove he is armed.

And the cops:

"Let the woman go. Let her come out."

Crash, bang. The woman leaves.

She doesn't say, Bye-bye, Papito, or Good luck, or anything. There's a deafening nothingness in there, chez Papito. Even I can hear it, though it's hard to hear things that make no sound. I hear the nothingness and Papito's breathing isn't part of it, nor is his terror, nothing. Papito's terror must be immeasurable, though its waves don't reach me—how strange—as do those of the gas they are using to drown him.

Give up, they shout, kick, howl with fury. Give up. We'll count to three. Then we'll bust the door down and come in shooting.

To three, I say to myself, not much of a countdown for a man's life. Father, Son, and Holy Ghost, that's three, and what can Papito do with a trinity all to himself that ticks his life away?

One, they shout from outside, thinking themselves magnanimous. Be strong, Papito. And he must be running in circles in an apartment cramped as mine, at every window running into the invisible eye of a telescopic sight.

I don't turn on my lights, just in case. I put my cheek against the wall and I am with you, Papito, inside your skin.

Two, they shout at him at me and he answers: Don't try it. If you break in, I'll kill myself.

I almost didn't hear, three. The shot obliterated it and the astonished running feet and the splintering door and the silence.

A suicide right here, Papito. Now what's left for me? Just to sit on the floor with my head on my knees, hopeless, waiting for the smell of powder to vanish and your finger to loosen on the trigger.

So alone, Papito, and with me so nearby.

After all the scrambling, the calm following an irremediable act. I opened my door and poked my nose out, my head, my whole body, and I managed to sneak into the apartment next door without anybody noticing.

Forgettable Papito little-nothing was a rag tossed on the floor. They nudged him a bit with their boots, trussed him on a stretcher, covered him with a dirty blanket, and headed for the morgue.

A puddle of blood remained that had once been Papito. A sublime stain, the color of life.

In that stain, my neighbor was great. He was important. I leaned down and said to him:

"Shout your name to me and don't be afraid. I can get you a good lawyer."

And I got no answer, as usual.

tr. Christopher Leland

· *Open Door*

Strange

Things

Happen

Here

Strange

Things

Happen

Here

In the café on the corner—every self-respecting café is on a corner, every meeting place is a crossing of two paths (two lives)—Mario and Pedro each order a cup of black coffee and put lots of sugar in it because sugar is free and provides nourishment. Mario and Pedro have been flat broke for some time—not that they're complaining, but it's time they got lucky for a change—and suddenly they see the abandoned briefcase, and just by looking at each other they tell themselves that maybe the moment has come. Right here, boys, in the café on the corner, no different from a hundred others.

The briefcase is there all by itself on a chair leaning against the table, and nobody has come back to look for it. The neighborhood boys come and go, they exchange remarks that Mario and Pedro don't listen to. There are more of them every day and they have a funny accent, they're from the interior. I wonder what they're doing here, why they've come. Mario and Pedro wonder if someone is going to sit down at the table in the

back, move the chair, and find the briefcase that they almost
love, almost caress and smell and lick and kiss. A man finally
comes and sits down at the table alone (and to think that the
briefcase is probably full of money, and that guy's going to
latch onto it for the modest price of a vermouth with lemon,
which is what he finally asks for after taking a little while to
make up his mind). They bring him the vermouth, along with
a whole bunch of appetizers. Which olive, which little piece of
cheese will he be raising to his mouth when he spots the briefcase on the chair next to his? Pedro and Mario don't even want
to think about it and yet it's all they *can* think about. When all
is said and done the guy has as much or as little right to the
briefcase as they do. When all is said and done it's only a question of chance, a table more carefully chosen, and that's it. The
guy sips his drink indifferently, swallowing one appetizer or
another; the two of them can't even order another coffee because they're out of dough as might happen to you or to me,
more perhaps to me than to you, but that's beside the point
now that Pedro and Mario are being tyrannized by a guy who's
picking bits of salami out of his teeth with his fingernail as he
finishes his drink, not seeing a thing and not listening to what
the boys are saying. You see them on street corners. Even Elba
said something about it the other day, can you imagine, she's
so nearsighted. Just like science fiction, they've landed from
another planet even though they look like guys from the interior but with their hair so well combed, they're nice and neat I
tell you, and I asked one of them what time it was but didn't
get anywhere—they don't have watches, of course. Why
would they want a watch anyway, you might ask, if they live in
a different time from us? I saw them, too. They come out from
under the pavement in the streets and that's where they still are
and who knows what they're looking for, though we do know
that they leave holes in the streets, those enormous potholes
they come out of that can't ever be filled in.

· *Open Door*

The guy with the vermouth isn't listening to them, and neither are Mario and Pedro, who are worrying about a briefcase forgotten on a chair that's bound to contain something of value because otherwise it wouldn't have been forgotten just so they could get it, just the two of them, not the guy with the vermouth. He's finished his drink, picked his teeth, left some of the appetizers almost untouched. He gets up from the table, pays, the waiter takes everything off the table, puts tip in pocket, wipes table with damp cloth, goes off and, man, the time has come because there's lots going on at the other end of the café and there's nobody at this end and Mario and Pedro know it's now or never.

Mario comes out first with the briefcase under his arm and that's why he's the first to see a man's jacket lying on top of a car next to the sidewalk. That is to say, the car is next to the sidewalk, so the jacket lying on the roof is too. A splendid jacket, of stupendous quality. Pedro sees it too, his legs shake because it's too much of a coincidence, he could sure use a new jacket, especially one with the pockets stuffed with dough. Mario can't work himself up to grabbing it. Pedro can, though with a certain remorse, which gets worse and practically explodes when he sees two cops coming toward them to . . .

"We found this car on a jacket. This jacket on a car. We don't know what to do with it. The jacket, I mean."

"Well, leave it where you found it then. Don't bother us with things like that, we have more important business to attend to."

More crucial business. Like the persecution of man by man if you'll allow me to use that euphemism. And so the famous jacket is now in Pedro's trembling hands, which have picked it up with much affection. He sure needed a jacket like this one, a sports jacket, well lined, lined with cash not silk who cares about silk? With the booty in hand they head back home. They don't have the nerve to take out one of the crisp bills that Mario thought he had glimpsed when he opened the briefcase just a hair—spare change to take a taxi or a stinking bus.

They keep an eye peeled to see whether the strange things that are going on here, the things they happened to overhear in the café, have something to do with their two finds. The strange characters either haven't appeared in this part of town or have been replaced: two policemen per corner are too many because there are lots of corners. This is not a gray afternoon like any other, and come to think of it maybe it isn't even a lucky afternoon the way it appears to be. These are the blank faces of a weekday, so different from the blank faces on Sunday. Pedro and Mario have a color now, they have a mask and can feel themselves exist because a briefcase (ugly word) and a sports jacket blossomed in their path. (A jacket that's not as new as it appeared to be—threadbare but respectable. That's it: a respectable jacket.) As afternoons go, this isn't an easy one. Something is moving in the air with the howl of the sirens and they're beginning to feel fingered. They see police everywhere, police in the dark hallways, in pairs on all the corners in the city, police bouncing up and down on their motorcycles against traffic as though the proper functioning of the country depended on them, as maybe it does, yes, that's why things are as they are and Mario doesn't dare say that aloud because the briefcase has him tongue-tied, not that there's a microphone concealed in it, but what paranoia, when nobody's forcing him to carry it! He could get rid of it in some dark alley—but how can you let go of a fortune that's practically fallen in your lap, even if the fortune's got a load of dynamite inside? He takes a more natural grip on the briefcase, holds it affectionately, not as though it were about to explode. At this same moment Pedro decides to put the jacket on and it's a little too big for him but not ridiculous, no not at all. Loose-fitting, yes, but not ridiculous; comfortable, warm, affectionate, just a little bit frayed at the edges, worn. Pedro puts his hands in the pockets of the

· *Open Door*

jacket (*his* pockets) and discovers a few old bus tickets, a dirty handkerchief, several bills, and some coins. He can't bring himself to say anything to Mario and suddenly he turns around to see if they're being followed. Maybe they've fallen into some sort of trap, and Mario must be feeling the same way because he isn't saying a word either. He's whistling between his teeth with the expression of a guy who's been carrying around a ridiculous black briefcase like this all his life. The situation doesn't seem quite as bright as it did in the beginning. It looks as though nobody has followed them, but who knows: there are people coming along behind them and maybe somebody left the briefcase and the jacket behind for some obscure reason. Mario finally makes up his mind and murmurs to Pedro: Let's not go home, let's go on as if nothing had happened, I want to see if we're being followed. That's okay with Pedro. Mario nostalgically remembers the time (an hour ago) when they could talk out loud and even laugh. The briefcase is getting too heavy and he's tempted once again to abandon it to its fate. Abandon it without having had a look at what's inside? Sheer cowardice.

They walk about aimlessly so as to put any possible though improbable tail off the track. It's no longer Pedro and Mario walking, it's a jacket and a briefcase that have turned into people. They go on walking and finally the jacket says: "Let's have a drink in a bar. I'm dying of thirst."

"With all this? Without even knowing where it came from?"

"Yeah, sure. There's some money in one pocket." He takes a trembling hand with two bills in it out of the pocket. A thousand nice solid pesos. He's not up to rummaging around in the pockets anymore, but he thinks—he smells—that there's more. They could use a couple of sandwiches, they can get them in this café that looks like a nice quiet place.

A guy says and the other girl's name is Saturdays there's no bread; anything, I wonder what kind of brainwashing . . . In turbulent times there's nothing like turning your ears on, though the bad thing about cafés is the din of voices that drowns out individual voices.

Listen, you're intelligent enough to understand.

They allow themselves to be distracted for a little, they too wonder what kind of brainwashing, and if the guy who was called intelligent believes he is. If it's a question of believing, they're ready to believe the bit about the Saturdays without bread, as though they didn't know that you need bread on Saturday to make the wafers for mass on Sunday, and on Sunday you need some wine to get through the terrible wilderness of workdays.

When a person gets around in the world—the cafés—with the antennae up he can tune in on all sorts of confessions and pick up the most abstruse (most absurd) reasoning processes, absolutely necessary because of the need to be on the alert and through the fault of these two objects that are alien to them and yet possess them, envelop them, especially now when those boys come into the café panting and sit down at a table with a nothing's-been-happening-around-here expression on their faces and take out writing pads, open books, but it's too late: they bring the police in on their heels and of course books don't fool the keen-witted guardians of the law, but instead get them all worked up. They've arrived in the wake of the students to impose law and order and they do, with much pushing and shoving: your identification papers, come on, come on, straight out to the paddy wagon waiting outside with its mouth wide open. Pedro and Mario can't figure out how to get out of there, how to clear a path for themselves through the mass of humanity that's leaving the café to its initial tranquility. As one of the kids goes out he drops a little package at Mario's feet, and in a reflex motion Mario draws the package over with his foot and hides it behind the famous briefcase leaning against the chair. Suddenly he's scared: he thinks he's gotten crazy

· *Open Door*

enough to appropriate anything within reach. Then he's even
more scared: he knows he's done it to protect the kid, but what
if the cops take it into their heads to search *him*? They'd find a
briefcase with who-knows-what inside, an inexplicable package (suddenly it strikes him funny, and he hallucinates that the
package is a bomb and sees his leg flying through the air accom-
panied out of sympathy by the briefcase, which has burst and
is spilling out big counterfeit bills). All this in the split second
that it took to hide the little package, and after that nothing.
It's better to leave your mind a blank and watch out for tele-
pathic cops and things like that. And what was he saying to
himself a thousand years ago when calm reigned?—a brainwashing; a self-service brainwash so as not to give away what's
inside this crazy head of mine. The kids move off, carted off
with a kick or two from the bluecoats; the package remains
there at the feet of those two respectable-looking gentlemen,
gentlemen with a jacket and a briefcase (each of them with one
of the two). Respectable gentlemen or two guys very much
alone in the peaceful café, gentlemen whom even a club sand-
wich couldn't console now.

They stand up. Mario knows that if he leaves the little package, the waiter is going to call him back and the jig'll be up. He
picks it up, thus adding it to the day's booty but only for a short
while; with trembling hands he deposits it in a garbage can on
a deserted street. Pedro, who's walking next to him, doesn't
understand at all what's going on, but can't work up the
strength to ask.

At times, when everything is clear, all sorts of questions can
be asked, but in moments like this the mere fact of still being
alive condenses everything that is askable and diminishes its
value. All they can do is to keep walking, that's all they can do,
halting now and then to see for example why that man over
there is crying. And the man cries so gently that it's almost sacrilege not to stop and see what the trouble is. It's shop-closing

time and the salesgirls heading home are trying to find out what's wrong: their maternal instinct is always ready and waiting, and the man is weeping inconsolably. Finally he manages to stammer: I can't stand it anymore. A little knot of people has formed around him with understanding looks on their faces, but they don't understand at all. When he shakes the newspaper and says I can't stand it anymore, some people think that he's read the news and the weight of the world is too much for him. They are about to go and leave him to his spinelessness. Finally he manages to explain between hiccups that he's been looking for work for months and doesn't have one peso left for the bus home, nor an ounce of strength to keep on looking.

"Work," Pedro says to Mario. "Come on, this scene's not for us."

"Well, we don't have anything to give him anyway. I wish we did."

Work, work, the others chorus and their hearts are touched, because this word is intelligible whereas tears are not. The man's tears keep boring into the asphalt and who knows what they find, but nobody wonders except maybe him, maybe he's saying to himself, my tears are penetrating the ground and may discover oil. If I die right here and now, maybe I can slip through the holes made by my tears in the asphalt, and in a thousand years I'll have turned into oil so that somebody else like me, in the same circumstances . . . A fine idea, but the chorus doesn't allow him to become lost in his own thoughts, which—it surmises—are thoughts of death (the chorus is afraid: what an assault it is on the peace of mind of the average citizen, for whom death is something you read about in the newspapers). Lack of work, yes, all of them understand being out of a job and are ready to help him. That's much better than death. And the good-hearted salesgirls from the hardware stores open their purses and take out some crumpled bills, a

· *Open Door*

collection is immediately taken up, the most assertive ones take the others' money and urge them to cough up more. Mario is trying to open the briefcase—what treasures can there be inside to share with this guy? Pedro thinks he should have fished out the package that Mario tossed in the garbage can. Maybe it was work tools, spray paint, or the perfect equipment for making a bomb, something to give this guy so that inactivity doesn't wipe him out.

The girls are now pressing the guy to accept the money that's been collected. The guy keeps shrieking that he doesn't want charity. One of the girls explains to him that it's a spontaneous contribution to help his family out while he looks for work with better spirits and a full stomach. The crocodile is now weeping with emotion. The salesgirls feel good, redeemed, and Pedro and Mario decide that this is a lucky sign.

Maybe if they keep the guy company Mario will make up his mind to open the briefcase, and Pedro can search the jacket pockets to find their secret contents.

So when the guy is alone again they take him by the arm and invite him to eat with them. The guy hangs back at first, he's afraid of the two of them: they might be trying to get the dough he's just received. He no longer knows if it's true or not that he can't find work or if this is his work—pretending to be desperate so that people in the neighborhood feel sorry for him. The thought suddenly crosses his mind: if it's true that I'm a desperate man and everybody was so good to me, there's no reason why these two won't be. If I pretended to be desperate it means that I'm not a bad actor, and I'm going to get something out of these two as well. He decides they have an odd look about them but seem honest, so the three of them go off to a cheap restaurant together to offer themselves the luxury of some good sausages and plenty of wine.

Three, one of them thinks, is a lucky number. We'll see if something good comes of it.

Why have they spent all this time telling one another their life stories, which maybe are true? The three of them discover an identical need to relate their life stories in full detail, from the time when they were little to these fateful days when so many strange things are happening. The restaurant is near the station and at certain moments they dream of leaving or of derailing a train or something, so as to rid themselves of the tensions building up inside. It's the hour for dreaming and none of the three wants to ask for the check. Neither Pedro nor Mario has said a word about their surprising finds. And the guy wouldn't dream of paying for these two bums' dinners, and besides they invited him.

The tension becomes unbearable and all they have to do is make up their minds. Hours have gone by. Around them the waiters are piling the chairs on the tables, like a scaffolding that is closing in little by little, threatening to swallow them up, because the waiters have felt a sudden urge to build and they keep piling chairs on top of chairs, tables on top of tables, and chairs and then more chairs. They are going to be imprisoned in a net of wooden legs, a tomb of chairs and who knows how many tables. A good end for these three cowards who can't make up their minds to ask for the check. Here they lie: they've paid for seven sausage sandwiches and two pitchers of table wine with their lives. A fair price.

Finally Pedro—Pedro the bold—asks for the check and prays that the money in the outside pockets is enough to cover it. The inside pockets are an inscrutable world even here, shielded by the chairs; the inner pockets form too intricate a labyrinth for him. He would have to live other people's lives if he got into the inside pockets of the jacket, get involved with something that doesn't belong to him, lose himself by stepping into madness.

There is enough money. Friends by now, relieved, the three go out of the restaurant. Pretending to be absentminded,

· *Open Door*

Mario has left the briefcase—too heavy, that's it—amid the intricate construction of chairs and tables piled on top of each other, and he is certain it won't be discovered until the next day. A few blocks farther on, they say good-by to the guy and the two of them walk back to the apartment that they share. They are almost there when Pedro realizes that Mario no longer has the briefcase. He then takes off the jacket, folds it affectionately, and leaves it on top of a parked car, its original location. Finally they open the door of the apartment without fear, and go to bed without fear, without money, and without illusions. They sleep soundly, until Mario jumps up with a start, unable to tell whether the bang that has awakened him was real or a dream.

tr. Helen Lane

The Best

Shod

An invasion of beggars, but there's one consolation: no one lacks shoes, there are more than enough shoes to go around. Sometimes, it's true, a shoe has to be taken off some severed leg found in the underbrush, and it's of no use except to somebody with only one good leg. But this doesn't happen very often, usually corpses are found with both shoes intact. Their clothing on the other hand isn't usable. Ordinarily it has bullet holes, bloodstains, or is torn apart, or an electric cattle prod has left burns that are ugly and difficult to hide. So we don't count on the clothes, but the shoes are like new. Generally they're good, they haven't had much wear because their owners haven't been allowed to get very far in life. They poke out their heads, they start thinking (thinking doesn't wear out shoes), and after just a few steps their career is cut off.

That is to say, we find shoes, and since they're not always the size we need, we've set up a little exchange post in a vacant lot downtown. We charge only a few pesos for the service: you can't ask much from a beggar, but even so it does help to pay for maté and some biscuits. We earn real money only when we manage to have a real sale. Sometimes the families of the dead people, who've heard of us heaven knows how, ask us to sell them the dead man's shoes if we have them. The shoes are the only thing that they can bury, poor things, because naturally the authorities would never let them have the body.

It's too bad that a good pair of shoes drops out of circulation, but we have to live and we can't refuse to work for a good cause. Ours is a true apostolate and that's what the police think, too, so they never bother us as we search about in vacant lots, sewer conduits, fallow fields, thickets, and other nooks and crannies where a corpse may be hidden. The police are well aware that, thanks to us, this city can boast of being the one with the best-shod beggars in the world.

tr. Helen Lane

The Gift

of Words

I take tremendous pleasure in saying no to everything. Saying yes is easy, it makes people like you, it earns you a few smiles and then you can go ahead and do as you please. But it's saying no that gives you a defiant omnipotence that can be extolled only on the highest balconies, from which your *no* doesn't even reach those below in the main square. To teach humility to those who come to listen to me, I have ordered trenches dug in the square. So everything is in its proper place: the people at the lowest level, then the ground, above ground a few palm trees and other greenery, and me on top of it all saying *no* whenever the occasion arises, and that is often. They acclaim me from the trenches, I impart to them my benediction from above, and sometimes a pigeon transports it and lets it fall somewhat grotesquely on the head of one of my people. This must be borne in mind: my people are my public, and must

· *Open Door*

witness the monumental unfolding of our intentions (and occasionally our attentions), and with luck receive at certain special times our gift in the form of pigeon droppings.

They are the chosen ones. We limit ourselves to speaking, to making a vague eucharistic gesture from the balcony, and the pigeons take care of designating the handful of elect of the day. Those who receive the pigeon shit on the head (which is really good luck) are appointed ministers, those who can show pigeon shit on their lapels become the guardians of law and order (upon receiving the Order of Merit) and have carte blanche to beat up anyone who strikes them as suspicious, not likable, or sad. But it must also be kept in mind that this is not a post without risks: if the pigeon deposits its consecrative offering on the man who is beaten up, that's enough to reverse the roles and the former guardian of law and order becomes the victim.

It rather amuses me to watch these sights from my balcony, and that's why I ordered the roofless tunnels furrowing the plaza from east to west to be built. Everybody is neatly filed in them without disturbing the flower beds, and when they fight they don't raise too much dust. A fine people, I tell myself, being resolved to defend their interests as I see fit; they have earned the right to have toilets in their trenches, to be used when my speeches last more than eight hours.

At times I go over the long speeches with my prime minister, to see if they're counterproductive. It's quite true that they are a diversion for the people, who therefore think less or don't think at all, but it's also true that people don't work because of them and this weighs rather heavily upon me. The country has ground to a halt, one must admit, and even though my prime minister says that this is only a rest period—a necessary pause for people to catch their breath—at times I have my doubts. But when the young people in the square shout, "We're all for you, we adore you," then I think that with my words I must continue to keep them at fever pitch.

I have already made certain major, though hidden, changes in the balcony: a comfortable, upholstered chair has been set up for me, a high one in which, when seen from below, I appear to be standing up, and a well-concealed secret urinal to take care of my most urgent needs. My prime minister (whom henceforth we shall refer to as Pancho) insisted that the urinal empty onto the plaza, but I was opposed to the idea. His theory that the people receive everything that comes from me as a form of anointment may be true, but for now I prefer to move cautiously. That's me—a prudent man.

During the longest speeches my chief enemy is drowsiness—sometimes I fall asleep in the middle of a sentence. Those below wait anxiously and acclaim me, but I don't even hear them shouting. When I wake up I console them by saying:

"The torrent of my words will never run dry, it is an inexhaustible fountain with which I give sustenance to my people and I shall continue to nourish my people to the last drop of my life, which belongs to you. Like a cormorant that rends its own crop to feed its offspring, I shall sacrifice the last breath of my torn throat for the benefit of my people, who are my children."

It is moving to see how after phrases of this sort the enthusiasm of a gabbling anthill bubbles up in the trenches. It was for this reason that I did not agree to the proposal for transparent plastic awnings now that the rainy season is approaching. Pancho says it's a good idea, but I suspect that in this case Pancho is concealing some sort of shady business beneath his poncho. Because even if it's true that loudspeakers could be installed inside the trenches, and that at the same time I could see the people thanks to the transparent awnings, it would be impossible to hear them acclaiming me. It's their shouts of approval that make me go on running the country, and they alone arouse my eloquence. So I want no awnings, I want direct con-

· *Open Door*

tact, bodily contact with my people. I am told that down below they have everything perfectly organized: they have set up kitchens, first aid stations, and other necessary services. I am also told that certain brazen couples fornicate while I'm speaking, but I choose not to believe it, though the wave of births that mobilized them recently, just when I was beginning to deal with the problems of overpopulation and environmental pollution, gives me pause for thought. Tomorrow I shall preach them a real sermon on Divine Law and chastity. If they don't listen to me, they should at least fear Him.

Down below

They people experience moments of fear, it's true, especially now that the rainy season is upon us and the government has provided nothing to protect the trenches. The believers among them painfully make their way to the third trench to the north, where a priest has improvised an altar and imparts his benediction after receiving a modest contribution for the Virgin. They don't miss a trick, according to the atheists, who are content to stay where they are, hoping that at the last minute the government will take some measure to protect them from the torrential rain.

Like the multiple legs of centipedes, rumors of a conspiracy are also rampant. But this is no time to try to foment an uprising of the masses, and the rebels know this: the Leader has begun a speech marathon and no one wants to miss a single word or lose his place in the trenches. Soldiers are distributing food, trucks full of corn have arrived, and in the kitchens various specialties are being prepared: tamales, mute, tortillas, locro.

A few pessimists (there are always dissenters) say that the corn harvest will run out soon, and since no one has tilled the fields since the Leader began speaking, they'll be left without food. They're making the usual mistake of thinking that the inhabitants of the capital are the whole population of the country. And what are the Indians for? ask the optimists. Even though no one is there to urge them on, the Indians will of course continue tilling the fields. They will plow, sow, harvest. This is now instinctive with them, and what's more they won't allow the poor city-dwellers to die of hunger simply because they've become an audience.

Moreover, thanks to widespread hunger and a certain gluttony, the people themselves have done away with the arbitrary hierarchization caused by pigeons. Ministers anointed by pigeons are a thing of the past, for there are no more pigeons in the main square: all have been roasted. A study is now being made of the possibility of breeding aseptic rats to increase the food value of the community stews.

This is discussed while the Leader rests or meets with his minister, because when the Leader speaks, the silence in the trenches is tomblike, to the point that fear of the coming of the rainy season is postponed until the next silence. And this is true even if the sky is already growing dark; they aren't going to abandon their posts just because of a few drops of water. The Leader speaks with growing warmth, and there's a good chance that his fiery eloquence will dry up the rain as it falls. But with the first heavy downpour they realize that this is a vain hope, and when the first severe storm begins (the first in a series that will last for three months) those in the trenches discover the existence of primordial mud, which soon comes up to their knees. The Leader's words tumble over each other, as do the people as they try to keep their balance in the mud. There are many deserters. Little by little the trenches empty out onto the square and people spill out from the square into the neighboring streets. What can they do but leave, even though it's hard for the people to abandon the warm voice of the Leader and the communal stewpots and the easy albeit restricting life of the trenches.

· *Open Door*

Luckily the Leader cannot see the cowardly retreat of his people, for the thick curtain of rain cuts off his vision. The people cannot see their Leader either, and that is why some stay behind floundering in the mud, and others go off with deep guilt feelings, unaware that the balcony has been empty for some time, and that the loudspeakers are broadcasting old recorded messages as the Leader, in his enormous bed, gargles with salt water in an effort to cure a loss of voice that threatens to become chronic.

tr. Helen Lane

Love

of

Animals

Blue car

Now that we've established that it's a person and not a spaniel, we proceed to the second question: man or woman? A long time goes by and we still haven't come up with an answer.

It'll get where it's going eventually. Not us—we're getting nowhere.

Ask us anything you like, the formula for sulphur trioxide or how to tie knots in worlds of an even number of dimensions, and we'll be able to answer. But don't ask us which sign is the right one: a little circle with an arrow pointing up, or a little circle with a cross below it, or just a plain little circle like a zero or an asshole. I say to Sebastián: look, old pal, we've got to come up with an answer one way or the other.

Wherever it's going it'll get there eventually, and it's discouraging for us not to know what sex it is, or rather what sex it would imagine itself to belong to or better still would give itself to.

Though sometimes of course the opposite one or the same

· *Open Door*

one . . . One look won't tell us that, however, and I say to Sebastián, step on it, old man, let's see if we can catch him / her.

All I get for an answer is shut your trap, you big prick, because he's glued to the steering wheel, but we start calling the mysterious character in the other car Lola. If it turns out to be a boy we'll call him Lalo, I think, and he'll be some dish because he's got a head of hair that makes you want to stick it in your mouth and suck it nice and slow like cotton candy—man, I must be a fairy, thinking of things like that—but I'm no queer, that's for sure, I'd far rather have it turn out to be Lola, not to mention having it close, like right here on my lap, and I say to Sebastián, Sebas old boy, step on it, it's getting away, and he does and clings to a curve following on the other one's tail and weaves in and out of the traffic cool as anything, zigzagging with real style 'cause that's what us B.A. cats are made for, leg holds and dribbling and kicks in the slats, sensational dodgers chasing after the greatest asses in all creation. Give it the lead foot, Sebas, put it right down to the floor, just look at it diving through there, it's asking for it. Lola or Lalo in that white job with the chauffeur—haul ass, man, we've gotta get a better look at the puss on that character.

White car

"Don't turn around. We're being followed."

"Maybe you're just imagining it. Make a sharp right. Still there?"

"Still there."

"Federal Coordination?"

"I don't think so. It's blue, all right, but an old model. And no antennae."

"Speed up and make it through the light. What are they up to?"

"They're going through the red light."

"Nobody's flagging them down?"

"No. A bad sign."

"Do you think they recognized me?"

"Not with that wig."

"How many are there?"

"Two."

"Could the other two be hiding in the backseat? Strange. Don't turn around, just keep watching in the rearview mirror. Make a sharp left the first chance you get. Are they still behind us?"

"Yes."

Blue car

Come on, man, floor it so we can catch up with 'em, it's worth it, listen, man, we can't just sit here with our asses hanging out and have somebody barge in ahead of us. Just look at that beauty go, and a chauffeur too, that must be some piece of tail, maybe a TV star. Must be scared of getting kidnapped, the little darling, Daddy's sweetie pie, but that's not what we've got in mind, baby doll, we wouldn't hurt a hair on your precious little head. Come on over here and let me lick you all over, honey. Hey, Sebas, don't get all hot and horny, come on, cool it, keep a good grip on that wheel, look at how it took that curve, how about that! Wow, just like her curves, exactly the same, how much you bet? What a bitch, that guy's not just a speed demon, he's a slalom expert. Come on, floor it, this cat's gonna catch you anyway, you little mouse. You stuck-up little rat, sitting there stiff as a board, not turning a hair. Come on, mouse, turn around, we want to see who you are.

And what if it turns out to be a stud instead of a chick? After all this chasing and risking getting a fistful of tickets—have a look and see if it's a stud and we'll shit all over him. With that head of hair though . . . But even if it's a guy we'll give it to him

· *Open Door*

anyway, because he's a stupid ass, making us chase after him like a couple of idiots. We'll let the chauffeur alone though, he's just a poor bastard doing his job. We can even hire him ourselves and spend the rest of our days chasing after a couple thousand broads that give us the slip. Hey, Sebas, don't get your feelings hurt, you're a real Fangio, man, come on, floor it, you're gaining on 'em.

White car

"Can't shake them. I'd say we're in bad trouble. Let's pull over and play dumb. Or put up a fight. We can't keep going forever, there's not much gas left. And going into the garage would be suicide."

"Parking would be even more suicidal, with everything we've got in here. I can't understand why they haven't turned on the siren—they'd have caught us long ago. And they don't seem to have radio equipment, do they?"

"I don't think so. Otherwise we'd have had patrol cars on our backs by now."

"Strange. They may be off duty. Make a sharp right!"

Blue car

Where the hell are they taking us? We're clear out in the boondocks! Listen, where're we headed, anyway? That one's sure playing hard to get. Careful! Make a right!

No one ever discovered why the occupants of the white car suddenly slowed down. They didn't live to explain why. The two men in the blue car, on the other hand, have more than enough time to explain; in jail they are subjected—endlessly—to what in those precincts are called "interrogations," but they haven't the slightest idea what to say, or what to make of the whole thing. Who were the two guys in the white car (so they were both guys, for Chrissake!), where were they headed, who were the guns for, where were they going, what were the two guys' names, what organization, who are the leaders, where were they headed, who were the guns for, what were the two guys' names, the two guys?

Reporting the news item in greater detail, the afternoon papers said that the terrorists' two cars (one blue, the other white) ended up a single twisted mass that was like a rosette in the Argentine national colors. As a sign of protest (though it is not known whether against the events or against the exaggerated metaphors of the local press), avant-garde painters immediately invented Crash-Art, and the first representative work of the school was entitled National Collision. The two men in the white car never knew that thanks to them a battered submachine gun came to be considered a work of art par excellence. The two men in the blue car don't give a damn about works of art.

tr. Helen Lane

The Verb

to Kill

He kills—he killed—he will kill—he has killed—he had killed—he will have killed—he would have killed—he is killing—he was killing—he has been killing—he would have been killing—he will have been killing—he will be killing—he would be killing—he may kill.

We decided that none of these tenses or moods suited him. Did he kill, will he kill, will he have killed? We think he *is* killing, with every step, with every breath, with every . . . We don't like him to get close to us but we come across him when we go clam-digging on the beach. We walk from north to south, and he comes from south to north, closer to the dunes, as if looking for pebbles. He looks at us and we look at him—did he kill, will he kill, would he have killed, is he killing? We put down the sack with the clams and hold each other's hand till he passes. He doesn't throw so much as one little pebble at us, he doesn't even look at us, but afterward we're too weak in the knees to go on digging clams.

The other day he walked by us and right afterward we found an injured sea gull on the beach. We took the poor thing home and on the way we told it that we were good, not like him, that it didn't have to be afraid of us, and we even covered it up with my jacket so the cold wind wouldn't hurt its broken wing. Later we ate it in a stew. A little tough, but tasty.

The next day we went back to run on the beach. We didn't see him and we didn't find a single injured sea gull. He may be bad, but he's got something that attracts animals. For example, when we were fishing: hours without a bite until he suddenly showed up and then we caught a splendid sea bass. He didn't look at our catch or smile, and it's good he didn't because he looked more like a murderer than ever with his long bushy hair and gleaming eyes. He just went on gathering his pebbles as though nothing were wrong, thinking about the girls that he has killed, will kill, kills.

When he passes by we're petrified—will it be our turn someday? In school we conjugate the verb *to kill* and the shiver that goes up our spine isn't the same as when we see him passing on the beach, all puffed up with pride and gathering his pebbles. The shiver on the beach is lower down in our bodies and more stimulating, like sea air. He gathers all those pebbles to cover up the graves of his victims—very small, transparent pebbles that he holds up to the sun and looks through from time to time so as to make certain that the sun exists. Mama says that if he spends all day looking for pebbles, it's because he *eats* them. Mama can't think about anything but food, but I'm sure he eats something else. The last breath of his victims, for example. There's nothing more nourishing than the last sigh, the one that brings with it everything that a person has gathered over the years. He must have some secret for trapping this essence that escapes his victims, and that's why he doesn't need

· *Open Door*

vitamins. My sister and I are afraid he'll catch us some night and kill us to absorb everything that we've been eating over the last few years. We're terribly afraid because we're well nourished, Mama has always seen to it that we eat balanced meals and we've never lacked for fruit or vegetables even though they're very expensive in this part of the country. And clams have lots of iodine, Mama says, and fish are the healthiest food there is even though the taste of it bores us but why should he be bored because while he kills his victims (always girls, of course) he must do those terrible things to them that my sister and I keep imagining, just for fun. We spend hours talking about the things that he does to his victims before killing them just for fun. The papers often talk about degenerates like him but he's one of the worst because that's all he eats. The other day we spied on him while he was talking to the lettuce he has growing in his garden (he's crazy as well as degenerate). He was saying affectionate things to it and we were certain it was poisoned lettuce. For our part we don't say anything to lettuce, we have to eat it with oil and lemon even though it's disgusting, all because Mama says it has lots of vitamins. And now we have to swallow vitamins for him, what a bother, because the better fed we are the happier we'll make him and the more he'll like doing those terrible things the papers talk about and we imagine, just before killing us so as to gulp down our last breath full of vitamins in one big mouthful. He's going to do a whole bunch of things so repulsive we'll be ashamed to tell anybody, and we only say them in a whisper when we're on the beach and there's nobody within miles. He's going to take our last breath and then he'll be as strong as a bull to go kill other little girls like us. I hope he catches Pocha. But I hope he doesn't do any of those repulsive things to her before killing her because she might like it, the dirty thing. I hope he kills her straightaway by plunging a knife in her belly. But he'll have his fun with us for a long time because we're pretty and he'll like our bodies and our voices when we scream. And we will scream and scream but nobody will hear us because he's going to take us to a place very far away and then he will put in our mouths that terrible thing we know he has. Pocha already told us about it— he must have an enormous thing that he uses to kill his victims.

An enormous one, even though we've never seen it. To show how brave we are, we tried to watch him while he made peepee, but he saw us and chased us away. I wonder why he didn't want to show it to us. Maybe it's because he wants to surprise us on our last day here and catch us while we're pure so's to get more pleasure. That must be it. He's saving himself for our last day and that's why he doesn't try to get close to us.

Not anymore.

Papa finally lent us the rifle after we asked and asked for it to hunt rabbits. He told us we were big girls now, that we can go out alone with the rifle if we want to, but to be careful, and he said it was a reward for doing so well in school. It's true we're doing well in school. It isn't hard at all to learn to conjugate verbs:

He will be killed—he is killed—he has been killed.

tr. Helen Lane

· *Open Door*

All

About

Suicide

Ismael grabbed the gun and slowly rubbed it across his face. Then he pulled the trigger and there was a shot. Bang. One more person dead in the city. It's getting to be a vice. First he grabbed the revolver that was in a desk drawer, rubbed it gently across his face, put it to his temple, and pulled the trigger. Without saying a word. Bang. Dead.

Let's recapitulate: the office is grand, fit for a minister. The desk is ministerial too, and covered with a glass that must have reflected the scene, the shock. Ismael knew where the gun was, he'd hidden it there himself. So he didn't lose any time, all he had to do was open the right-hand drawer and stick his hand in. Then he got a good hold on it and rubbed it over his face with a certain pleasure before putting it to his temple and pulling the trigger. It was something almost sensual and quite unexpected. He hadn't even had time to think about it. A trivial gesture, and the gun had fired.

There's something missing: Ismael in the bar with a glass in his hand thinking over his future act and its possible consequences.

We must go back farther if we want to get at the truth: Ismael in the cradle crying because his diapers are dirty and nobody is changing him.

Not that far.

Ismael in the first grade fighting with a classmate who'll one day become a minister, his friend, a traitor.

No. Ismael in the ministry without being able to tell what he knew, forced to be silent. Ismael in the bar with the glass (his third) in his hand, and the irrevocable decision: better death.

Ismael pushing the revolving door at the entrance to the building, pushing the swinging door leading to the office section, saying good morning to the guard, opening the door of his office. Once in his office, seven steps to his desk. Terror, the act of opening the drawer, taking out the revolver, and rubbing it across his face, almost a single gesture and very quick. The act of putting it to his temple and pulling the trigger— another act, immediately following the previous one. Bang. Dead. And Ismael coming out of his office (the other man's office, the minister's) almost relieved, even though he can predict what awaits him.

tr. Helen Lane

· *Open Door*

The Celery

Munchers

I suppose I could ask them to stop munching celery at three o'clock in the morning, but that doesn't seem right. What with the price of celery these days. It's also possible that they munch celery as a sign of nonconformity and that they're joining housewives in protesting the price of vegetables. Or perhaps they're doing it out of a sense of superiority, to show that they can eat what others buy only as a luxury or to wear as boutonnieres.

There are three of them and they sometimes eat in unison or counterpoint. The noise in the basement where we live is almost terrifying. The greengrocer, our boss, sleeps with us too, he's a thrifty man, and the first night he woke up with a start, thinking that rats were eating the merchandise. It was all right for them to eat us, but the merchandise. . . . The rats leave us in peace though—they prefer the chick-peas. Now and then we give them a handful and they look grateful. The grocer doesn't know it—any gesture of generosity or waste gets him down. But the Celery Munchers chew with relish in the knowledge that they're consuming perishable merchandise—and besides, after the latest hike in prices almost nobody eats celery anymore, and the vegetable man would have to throw out the unsold celery if it weren't for three of his helpers—I'm not one of them of course—who get paid partly in celery. There's going to be a problem though when the celery runs out. The only other vegetables I know that make noise when you chew them are carrots, which they don't like, and radishes, which aren't half as good for the blood as celery.

Our boss is a heavy sleeper and acquires new habits easily, so the crunch-crunch of the Celery Munchers doesn't wake him up anymore. He stretches out on a pile of potatoes, covered with dirt, and ignores the sound of the human crushing machine. The Celery Munchers don't sleep much, their resistance to sleep is surprising; maybe it's due to some unknown property of celery. In any event the boss doesn't wake up anymore and the rhythmical chewing of the Celery Munchers puts me to sleep. You might say that our life is lived amid the green peace of garden vegetables, except for the neighbors' anxieties hanging over our heads. The grocery store is in the basement of a thirteen-story building, and in some strange way vibrations of fear filter down to us from the thirteen stories above. If only we knew what caused them, we might be able to attend some secret tenants' meeting. But these meetings take place in the locked laundry room at the top of the building and we belong to the basement. We don't have access to the terraces and that's why we're pasty white, the color of a turnip; if we don't even have the luxury of a little jaunt in an elevator, how can we know what goes on in tenants' meetings? The boss doesn't worry about such petty details: the elevators give him claustrophobia, the tenants' meetings make him sick, and moreover he's afraid that the owner will raise the rent if he sees him (that's why the boss doesn't bathe, so as to make himself

· *Open Door*

practically indistinguishable from the potatoes). The store is doing well and is open all day, Sundays and holidays included. We don't complain because the longer it stays open the better ventilated the basement is and the less time we spend smelling the boss, but the rumors that trickle down to us disturb our sleep.

A search warrant is only a piece of paper but here we are, hoping that they stumble upon the truth by themselves because our protestations of innocence aren't getting us anywhere. The police arrived with the warrant and right away turned everything topsy-turvy: they overturned crates of fruit, rummaged like madmen in the barrels of chick-peas, uncorked the few bottles of wine that were left and drank them, claiming that they had to see what was inside, stamped on the potatoes, the onions, the turnips, and the celery (the Celery Munchers wept). They broke open the pumpkins to see if they had been hollowed out inside, and shook the carrots hoping they were mikes or heaven knows what. And screaming, "You've been turned in! You've been turned in!" they smashed everything in sight.

It's true that a number of bombs have gone off in the neighborhood, but what can they be searching for in the grocery store? Imagine: they started by cautiously picking up each piece of fruit, holding it up to the light, and examining it, listening to it with a stethoscope. Then their fury mounted till it finally found its natural form of expression, which is kicking. First they kicked the fruit and then us a few times, until they realized that we had no hidden arms there, no gunpowder cache, nor were we digging secret tunnels or hiding terrorists or maintaining a people's jail behind a mountain of potatoes.

There was nothing at all, but we're in jail nonetheless. The boss cried—more for the lost merchandise than his lost freedom. The police refused to pay damages and now claim that the boss has to pay for cleaning their sticky boots. The Celery Munchers wept too; they're already showing alarming symptoms because of the lack of celery in their bloodstreams. This has been not only a moral disaster but an economic one as well and I demanded an explanation; finally the chief of police released us and that was how we found out about the neighbors' turning us in: they thought we were undermining the building. At three o'clock in the morning, every morning. A noise like a train moving that didn't stop even after we were hauled in. In short, the Celery Munchers had been replaced by rats who quickly polished off the damaged merchandise.

The building has now been shored up, and calm restored. The Celery Munchers are running around loose but are muzzled at night. The rats are in jail. Rumor has it that they're being used for strange experiments, to torture political prisoners; the experiments won't get very far, because they're macrobiotic pacifist rats. We miss them, but we're reluctant to ask to have them returned to us because we don't want them back contaminated.

tr. Helen Lane

· *Open Door*

Vision
out of
the Corner
of One Eye

It's true, he put his hand on my ass and I was about to scream bloody murder when the bus passed by a church and he crossed himself. He's a good sort after all, I said to myself. Maybe he didn't do it on purpose or maybe his right hand didn't know what his left hand was up to. I tried to move farther back in the bus—searching for explanations is one thing and letting yourself be pawed is another—but more passengers got on and there was no way I could do it. My wiggling to get out of his reach only let him get a better hold on me and even fondle me. I was nervous and finally moved over. He moved over, too. We passed by another church but he didn't notice it and when he raised his hand to his face it was to wipe the sweat off his forehead. I watched him out of the corner of one eye, pretending that nothing was happening, or at any rate not making him think I liked it. It was impossible to move a step farther and he began jiggling me. I decided to get even and put my hand on his behind. A few blocks later I got separated from him by a bunch of people. Then I was swept along by the passengers getting off the bus and now I'm sorry I lost him so suddenly because there was only 7,400 pesos in his wallet and I'd have gotten more out of him if we'd been alone. He seemed affectionate. And very generous.

tr. Helen Lane

Ladders

to Success

Don't you think you might have to rent a ladder? We must make everyone equal by working from the bottom up, we've been told, and there's no doubt that we all aspire to rise higher, but we don't always have our own means to reach the top, so sometimes we need the right kind of ladder. Our factory offers you all kinds, from the humble painter's ladder to the sumptuous royal one made from a single piece of wood. A well-carved piece of wood, of course, rosewood or ironwood (to iron out problems!) for bossy wives like mine. Though authoritarianism is not allowed in our plants, where, to be sure, the verticality prevails that we've heard so much about. From a practical point of view we don't quite know what the word means, but when it comes to ladders verticality is the norm. At one time we tried to manufacture horizontal ladders in order to make things on the same level equal, but the workers rebelled and went on strike, protesting health hazards and ideological deviations. We made no great effort to win them over because we realized that there wasn't much demand for horizontal ladders at retail outlets, not even to rent. Obviously, everybody aspires to climb, scale, ascend, and would have nothing to do with cautiously advancing along one level.

The first horizontal ladder that we made I took home to my wife as a present, but she didn't even bother to find out how it worked, and promptly converted it into a flowerpot holder. My wife always discourages me in my boldest undertakings. She's not always right—as for instance when she firmly opposed the manufacture of ladders to go down. She said that nobody would buy them because they required holes in the ground and few people have holes in the ground in their homes. The poor woman has no imagination: she can't see that the main square is full of opposition party members who try to go down when the government insists they go up. While the descending ladders were in fashion, the factory prospered and we were able to branch out: revolving ladders. They're the most expensive kind because they're run by motor, but they're ideal for getting rid of unwanted guests. You invite them upstairs, and centrifugal force does the rest. With these revolving stairways we managed to get rid of many creditors, but my wife, who's always thrifty, banished revolving ladders from our home and the factory, claiming that they used too much electricity.

We still get orders from the interior. We send out folding ladders that fit inside an envelope instead. But unfortunately I had to admit defeat and even though I've told this story in the present tense, it's a thing of the past. My wife thought it was too secular an activity once she'd converted me to the Church of Ladder-Day Saints.

tr. Helen Lane

· *Open Door*

A Story

About

Greenery

Walls have been built to contain the pampas but once upon a time a little seed outdid all those massed tons of cement, even though the verb *to outdo* is highly subjective and permits a vast range of interpretations. The objective fact is this: the walls don't let even a breath of pampas greenery through but they can't keep the wind from stealing in through the crevices. The wind is individualistic and thistle seeds are stubborn, and one finally managed to float windborne through the air and land in the urban zone. Today we can see a thistle thriving in a city that has eradicated green by decree.

In the beginning it was easy. People avoided looking down as they turned the corner, but now that the thistle has grown—favored by rains so surprising at this time of year—it's no longer so easy to avoid that sight, especially for those who work in the nearby skyscrapers and can't help but be dazzled as they cast a sidelong glance at its green radiance.

The mayor is fit to be tied. He thinks of all the money spent to change the traffic lights so that they turn from red to blue, and now this . . .

(Nobody has the courage to yank the thistle out, even with welding glasses on, for fear of being contaminated by the color or attacked by prickles.)

A new decree has just appeared in the *Official Journal*, stating that unofficially everything is permitted us, provided it doesn't lead to abuses. In this way they hope that some self-abnegating citizen will rid us of the thistle. This business about abuses sounds fishy; since it can be interpreted most any way, it's better to stick to the old procedures until we get clearer instructions. But most citizens feel liberated, a sensation almost unknown to those under fifteen.

The state of war began in the sixties, and it was never officially ended for the simple reason that it had never been officially declared. It's rumors that hang heaviest over us—rumors engendered by fear, and phrases that sometimes begin as an innocent joke then grow until they claim a great many victims. Perhaps the best example is the color that's now unmentionable: it all began because someone let it be known that the president didn't like being thought a gr . . . horn in politics. Then his successor had a daughter skinny as a rail who didn't look good in gr . . . , so it was declared unfashionable. After a while the wife of a minister was seen with another man in a park, and immediately parks, squares, and other gr . . . spaces were eliminated from the federal district. Then the mayor I referred to earlier came along and proscribed the pampas for reasons that were never explained, and finally the color of the traffic lights was changed and everything would be right except for the thistle. It disturbs many people; it evokes memories. There are even those who allow themselves to become nostalgic about billiard tables or the hypothetical benefits of chlorophyll. All on account of a prickly, ugly little thistle, which even so looks radiantly beautiful to many. Moreover, a

· *Open Door*

secret sect has sprung up with the thistle as its emblem, and its members have recently been in contact with Scotch separatists—can you imagine? They began by pursuing noble ends: freedom from discrimination on the basis of color or religion, and social justice and equality of the sexes. Little by little they've become fanatics. Now they say that if they win they'll make all citizens wear green uniforms, and the national beverage will be a soft drink made from green maté syrup.

The government already feels certain affinities with this dissident group and there is talk of an alliance soon. Meanwhile large groups of citizens make pilgrimages to the sacred thistle and bring it offerings of animal manure obtained on the black market. They have taken the clever precaution of covering the thistle with a white cloth so as not to be dazzled by it, and are organizing processions and singing hymns in the hope of an amnesty that will allow them to revere the thistle as a great monument to national harmony.

tr. Helen Lane

The Place

of Its

Quietude

All moon, all year,
all day, all wind
comes by and passes on.
All blood arrives
at the place of its quietude.
(Books of Chilam-Balam)

The altars have been erected in the country but the vapors reach us (those of us who live in the city, in the suburbs, those among us who believe that we can save ourselves). Those from the countryside have accepted their fate and are praying. Yet there's no visible motive for panic, only the usual shootings, police raids, customary patrols. But they must be dimly aware that the end is at hand. So many things are so confused now that the abnormal is imitating the natural and vice versa. The sirens and the wind, for example: the police car sirens are like the howling of the wind, with an identical sound and an identical power of destruction.

To keep a better watch on the inhabitants of the houses, a

· *Open Door*

type of siren is being used in the helicopters that is so high-pitched and strident that it makes the roofs fly off. Luckily the government has not yet found the formula for controlling those who don't live in single houses or on the top floors of high buildings. And there are very few of these: since the electricity has been cut off nobody ventures beyond the third floor because of the danger of stairways, the hideout of malefactors.

We must add that as consolation many who lost their roofs have had them replaced with Plexiglas skylights, gifts of the government. Above all in rural areas, where the straw roofs frequently fall off not only because of the sirens but also because of windstorms. That's what they're like in the country: they put up with anything, even with remaining where they are and setting up altars and organizing prayer meetings when time and weather permit. They have little time for prayer, and bad weather. The southeast wind blows out their votive candles, and floods demand their constant attention to keep the livestock (goats, sheep, pigs, a very few cows, and a fair number of chickens) from drowning. Fortunately they haven't had the nerve to come to the city as they did seven years ago, during that historic drought, when thirsty men flocked to the cities in search of water, trampling the parched bodies of those who had died along the way. But the city was not a solution either because the city dwellers didn't want them and drove them off with sticks like howling dogs, and they had to take refuge in the sea in water up to their waists, safe from the rocks hurled from the shore by those defending their bread, their drinking water, and their feeble dignity.

They aren't going to make the same mistake; even though this didn't happen here but in a neighboring country, it amounts to the same thing because while their individual memory is fragile their collective memory is enviable and comes to the surface to get them out of difficulties. Nonetheless we don't believe that the rebirth of religious sentiment will save them from what's happening now; it won't save them, but perhaps it will save us city dwellers who know how to sniff the air for a breath of copal incense that reaches us from the interior. They have great difficulty importing copal incense and we may be the ones to reap the benefits. Exhaust gases permitting, we do our best to breathe great lungfuls of incense—we know it's useless—just in case. That's the way everything is now: we have nothing to fear yet we're afraid. This is the best of all possible worlds, as they keep reminding us over the radio, and the way other worlds will be; the country is on its way to the future, and secret agents of aberrant ideologies can do nothing to halt its march, the government says, so in order to survive we pretend that we believe it. Leaving aside those who are working in the underground—there are few of them—our one hint of rebellion is the surreptitious sniffing of the air in search of something that comes to us from the countryside and shows up our lack of faith. I believe—I can't be sure, the subject is discussed furtively—that in certain suburban districts of the city groups of pilgrims are being formed to go to the interior to try to understand—and to justify—this new mythical tendency. We were never fervent believers and suddenly now we feel the need to set up altars. There must be something behind all this. In the café today with my friends—so you won't think we're in really bad straits, I might mention that friends can still get together in a café—very cautiously we touched upon the subject (we must always be careful, since the walls have ears) of what's going on in the interior. Has excessive fear brought them back to a primitive search for hope, or are they plotting something? Jorge suspects that the copal has hallucinogenic powers and they deprive themselves of many things in order to get it. It appears that copal cannot be transported by mechanical means, so it must come from Central America on the back of a mule or a man. Relays to transport it have already been organized and we might suspect that ammunition or at

· *Open Door*

least drugs or instructions arrive inside the bags of copal bark, if it weren't for the fact that our customs officials are so alert and clear-thinking. The local customs, of course, don't permit copal to enter the cities. We don't want it here either, although certain dissident intellectuals have declared our city an area of psychological catastrophe. But we have much more burning questions confronting us and we can't waste time on speeches and lectures on so-called metaphysics. Jorge says it's something much more profound. Jorge says, Jorge says . . . All we can do in cafés nowadays is talk, because in many of them we're no longer allowed to write, even though we keep ordering food and drink. They claim that they need the tables, but I suspect that those café owners who suppress the written word are really agents provocateurs. The idea started, I think, in the café at the corner of Paraguay and Pueyrredón, and spread through the city like a trail of lighted gunpowder. Now no writing is permitted in the cafés near the Mint, nor in some along the Avenida do Río Branco. In Pocitos yes, all the cafés allow writing and intellectuals gather there around 6:00 P.M. So long as it isn't a trap, as Jorge says, set up by the extremists, of course, since the government is above such machinations—in fact, above everyone in their helicopters, safeguarding the peace of the nation.

Nothing to fear. The escalation of violence only touches those who are looking for it, not us humble citizens who don't allow ourselves so much as a wry face or the least sign of discontent. (Of consternation yes, and there's good reason when they blow the roof off the house and sometimes the top of one's head as well, when they frisk us for arms in the street, or when the smell of copal becomes too intense and makes us feel like running to see what's up. Like running and running; acting absurdly is not always cowardice.)

We've finally become used to the smell of incense, which often competes with the smell of gunpowder, and now something else is coming our way: the distant sound of a flute. In the beginning we thought it was ultrasonic waves to break up demonstrations, but that wasn't it. The flute note is sustained, and to those not paying much attention it may sound like a lament; in reality it's a persistent melody that makes us lift our heads as in the old days when the roar of helicopters drew our attention. We have lost our capacity for amazement. We don't dance to that tune, nor do we break into a run when the patrols arrive from all directions and converge on top of us.

Sirens like the wind, flutes like ultrasonic notes to break up riots. It would appear that those in the interior have decided to borrow certain devices from the central power. At least that's what they're saying on the street, but it's never specified who those in the interior are: riffraff, provincials, foreign agents, groups of armed guerrillas, anarchists, researchers. That flute sound coming on top of the smell of incense is just too much. We might speak of sensorial and ideological infiltration, if in some remote corner of our national being we didn't feel that it's for our own good—a form of redemption. And this vague sensation restores to us the luxury of being afraid. Well no, not fear expressed aloud as in other times. The fear now is behind closed doors, silent, barren, with a low vibration that emerges in fits of temper on the streets or conjugal violence at home.

We have our nightmares and they are always of torture even though the times are not right for these subtleties. In the past they could spend time applying the most refined methods to extract confessions, but now confessions have been consigned to oblivion: everyone is guilty now, so on to something else. In our anachronistic dreams we city people still cling to tortures, but those in the interior don't dream or have nightmares: they've managed, we are told, to eliminate those hours of total surrender when the sleeper is at the mercy of his adversary. They fall into profound meditation for brief periods and keep nightmares at a distance; and the nightmares are limited to the

· *Open Door*

urban community. But we shouldn't talk of fear. So little is known—we know the advantage of silence. What do those in the interior do, for example, in front of their altars? We don't believe that they pray to the god invoked so often by the government, or that they've discovered new gods or resurrected the old ones. It must be something less obvious. Bah. These things shouldn't worry us, we live within four walls (often without a roof or with a skylight)—men addicted to asphalt. If they want to burn themselves on incense, let them; if they want to lose their breath blowing into an Indian flute, let them. None of that interests us. None of that can save us. Perhaps only fear, a little fear that makes us see our urban selves clearly. But we should not allow ourselves to experience fear because with a breath of fear so many other things come our way: questioning, horror, doubt, dissent, disgust. Let those far away in the fields or in the mountains show a great interest in useless practices if they like. We can always take a boat and go away; they are anchored in one spot and that's why they sing psalms.

Our life is quiet enough. Every once in a while a friend disappears, or a neighbor is killed, or one of our children's schoolmates—or even our own children—falls into a trap, but that isn't as apocalyptic as it seems; on the contrary, it's rhythmic and organic. The escalation of violence—one dead every twenty-four hours, every twenty-one, every eighteen, every fifteen, every twelve—ought not to worry us. More people die in other parts of the world, as that deputy said moments before he was shot. More, perhaps, but nowhere so close at hand as here.

When the radio speaks of the peace that reigns (television has disappeared—no one wants to show his face), we know it's a plea for help. The speakers are aware that bombs await them at every corner; they arrive at the station with their faces concealed, so when they walk the streets as respectable citizens, no one will recognize them. No one knows who attacks the speakers—after all, they only read what others write. But where do they write it? Under police surveillance and in custody? That makes sense. Science fiction writers foresaw the present state of affairs years ago and the government is now trying to keep new prophecies from proliferating (although certain members of the government—the less imaginative among them—have suggested allowing writers freedom of action so as to lift interesting ideas from them). I don't go along with such maneuvers, which is why I've devised an ingenious system for writing in the dark. I keep my manuscripts in a place that only I know about; we'll see what happens. Meanwhile the government bombards us with optimistic slogans that I don't repeat because they're all so familiar, and this is our only source of culture. Despite which I continue to write and try to be law-abiding and not

Last night I heard a strange noise and immediately hid my manuscript. I don't remember what I was going to jot down; I suspect it's not important anymore. I'm glad I have quick reflexes because suddenly someone turned the master switch, all the lights came on, and a squad of police entered to search the house. It'll take poor Betsy a week to put everything back in order, to say nothing of what they broke or what they must have taken away. Gaspar can't console her, but at least nothing more serious has happened than the search. The police questioned them as to why they had taken me in as a boarder, but they gave an adequate explanation and luckily, as if by a miracle, they didn't find my little board painted in phosphorescent colors so that I can write in the dark. I don't know what would have happened to me, Betsy, and Gaspar if they'd found it all; my hiding place is ingenious and I wonder whether it might not be better to hide something more useful in it. Well, it's too late to change now; I have to keep walking along this path of ink and tell the story of the doorman. I was at a tenants' meet-

· *Open Door*

ing and saw the single women mentally licking their chops when the new doorman was described: thirty-four years old and a bachelor. In the days that followed I saw him lavishing a lot of extra care on the bronze fittings at the main entrance and also reading a book while on duty. But I wasn't there when the police took him away. Rumor has it that he was an infiltrator from the interior. I know now that I should have talked with him, perhaps I would finally have understood something, untangled some of the threads of the plot. What are they doing in the interior, what are they after? I'd be hard put to say which of the single women in the building turned him in. They all look spiteful and perhaps have reason to, but are they all capable of running to the telephone and condemning someone out of spite? The radio gently urges us so often to inform, that they may even have felt they were doing their duty. I can now write all this down with a certain impunity, since I know I'm safe in my hiding place. That's why I can afford the luxury of writing a few stories. I even have the titles: "The Best Shod," "Strange Things Happen Here," "Love of Animals," "The Gift of Words." They're only for me, but if we're lucky enough to survive all this, perhaps they'll bear witness to the truth. Anyway they console me. And with the way I've worked it out, I have no fear of playing their game or giving them ideas. I can even do away with the subterfuge of referring to myself in the plural or in the masculine. I can be myself. Only I want it known that even though I'm a little naive and sometimes given to fantasy, not everything I've recorded is false. Certain things are true: the sound of the flute, the smell of incense, the sirens. It's also true that strange things are happening in the interior of the country and that I'd like to make common cause with them. It's true that we are—I am—afraid.

I'm writing secretly, and to my relief I've just learned that those in the interior are also writing. By the light of the votive candles they're writing the book of our people. This is a form of illusion for us and also a condemnation: when a people writes for itself, it is dying out and nothing can be done about it.

Some make light of this bit of information: they say we city dwellers have no connection with people of the interior, that we all descend from immigrants. I don't see how coming from somewhere else can be a reason to be proud when the very air we breathe, the sky and the landscape when there's a drop of sky or landscape left, are impregnated with them—those who have always lived here and have nourished the earth with their bodies. And it's said that they're now writing the book and it's hoped that this task will take many long years. Their memory is eternal and they have to go a long way back in time to arrive at the origin of the myth, dust the cobwebs off it, and demythicize it (in order to restore to the truth its essence, to take off its disguise). They say that we'll still have time to go on living, to create new myths for them. The pragmatists are in the city, the idealists are far away. Where will they meet?

Meanwhile the persecutions grow more insidious. One can't go out in the street without seeing men in uniform breaking the law for the mere pleasure of laughing at those who must obey it.

Though I'm quiet these days, I go on jotting it all down in bold strokes (and at great risk) because it's the only form of freedom left. Others still make enormous efforts to believe the radio, which transmits information quite different from what is already public knowledge. This clever system of contradictory messages is designed to drive the population mad; to preserve my sanity, I write in the dark without being able to reread what I've written. At least I feel that I'm supported by my fellow countrymen in the interior. I'm not writing a book like them, but it's something. Mine is a modest contribution and I hope it never gets into the hands of readers: I don't want to be discovered. Sometimes I return home so impressed by people

· *Open Door*

who wander blindly in the streets—people who have been beaten, mutilated, bloodied, or crippled—that I can't even write. But that doesn't matter. Nothing would happen if I stopped writing. If the people in the interior stopped writing—history would stop for us, disaster overcome us. They must have begun their story with the earliest times; one has to be patient. If they go on writing they may someday reach the present and overcome it, in all the meanings of the verb *to overcome*: leave it behind them, modify it, and with a little luck even improve it. It's a question of language.

tr. Helen Lane

The

Heretics

The Door

The first days of July brought cold winds and the ominous threat of a harsh winter to Santiago del Estero. A mass of gray dust floated in the air, and each gust seemed to bend the withered trees to the breaking point. Only the tall cactuses maintained their spiny, uniform profiles erect against the hurricane, until they also fell, just to demonstrate how hollow they were inside, how empty was their show of strength. The pale dust had bleached the landscape. The cold that slid through the skeletons of dead animals was made more unbearable by the sounds of splitting canvas and crackling thorny bushes.

Inside the hut, the wind raced mercilessly, as if across an open field. It didn't help to shut the carved door. The straw roof, the walls of tin and canvas were poor protection. Huddled around a dying fire, Orosmán, Belisaria, the eight children, and the grandmother sought warmth from each other rather than from the smoldering coals. The fourteen-month-old baby cried in the crate that served as a crib, and Belisaria asked herself what they would do with the newborn when it arrived. From the depths of the silence, she heard the voice of her oldest child, Orestes:

"We can't go on like this, Papa. Let's go to Tucumán. . . ."

"To Tucumán, to Tucumán," the children chorused.

"They say there are lights in the city. And the houses are tall and strong; no wind cuts through them."

And Orestes again:

"Don Zoilo says we'll find work there. They need many hands for the sugar. He says there's a lot of money."

"Papa, Don Zoilo went to the sugar harvest last year. He says that now he's too old to go back and that he'll sell you his cart."

"Orestes says we can exchange it for the goats and the two sheep. We won't need them there."

Orosmán protested, "How are we going to go, with Mama the way she is, eh?"

Belisaria paid no attention. "I'll go just the same."

"But Grandmother is old now."

"I also want to get warm, I want to be comfortable in my old age."

That night sleep came much easier to the family in the hut, with hope covering them like a shawl.

The following morning they were bursting with activity. First the discussion with Don Zoilo, who, in addition to the goats and the two sheep, wanted their door as well, an impossible demand. To part with the door was to betray all tradition. The door had five devils carved on it, and an angel above to frighten them. Actually, the angel looked more devilish than the devil himself. But that was the fault of Orosmán's grandfather, who had made the door back in the mission without knowing how to carve in wood. Nevertheless, the priests had told him that the door was very beautiful, and they had said, "Let's use it in the chapel." Instead of feeling proud, the grandfather had made off for the country that same night,

· *Open Door*

leading his horse with the door loaded on its back, because he did not want the door to be for God, but for himself and his kin. Among his kin it had remained, and Orosmán would not be the one to exchange it for a miserable roofless cart made from thick tree trunks, not even if it were the best cart in Santiago.

Finally, with the delivery of the animals, the deal was concluded and the cart changed owners. The horses neighed happily under the weight of harnesses that had lain unused in a corner of the hut for five years. The long rawhide laces stroked their flanks to brush away flies, and they felt a new vigor.

Orosmán and the children loaded the sacks of corn, along with everything they could find in the hut. Little by little the cart filled up, until the entire hut was piled there. The burlap walls were used to wrap belongings, and the straw from the roof was stuffed in to fill gaps and to make mattresses. Finally, only two posts remained standing, like a cross above the tomb of the little hut to which they would never return.

Don Zoilo, squatting on the ground and sipping maté, said to them, "Take my advice, go directly to the city. They'll take better care of you there. You'll get better pay. Don't take work in the country, go to the city."

Such were his words of farewell. Orosmán, mounted on the middle horse, cracked the whip, and they were off. On the open road, a cold night caught them by surprise and forced them to halt. They warmed some food on the fire made wispy by the wind, and then slept buried in the cart between bundles and straw. The following morning brought them a little sun, like a promise, and led them to the road that went directly to the city. Behind them was the thorny and dry slope, but the landscape, at each step more arid, refused to change. As the afternoon slipped away, the sky began to take on ugly tones of gray until landscape and sky merged in a haze at the horizon. Night returned to cover them, their hunger, and their cold.

When they began moving again, they could see green at the sides of the road, planted fields: the city was near now. Suddenly a roar jolted them out of their weariness. Another followed, then still another.

"Cannons," said Orestes in a hushed voice. "That's how they told me cannons sound: they make everything tremble."

"Don't talk nonsense, my son. It must be the noise of the big city," and he whipped the horses to quicken the pace.

The road into the city was lined with houses and gardens, and there were swarms of people hurrying toward the center of town. The cart followed the crowd, circled a plaza, then plunged straight ahead through a narrow street. Suddenly, as they turned a corner, they caught sight of a platoon of soldiers and heard a commanding voice give the order to march.

They continued moving ahead. The tall buildings were covered with flags, sky blue and white, and the crowd was getting larger, multiplying itself into all the people in the world who couldn't stop shouting and singing. Cars and surreys pushed the cart toward the main plaza, and Orosmán and his family, bewildered, let themselves be carried along. The tanks advancing toward them only made their frightened eyes grow larger, and to top it off, there was a policeman who shouted, "Keep moving, keep moving, you can't stop here."

The drums of the band were striking an ever faster beat, and the cart was being dragged into the current. A mounted sergeant approached them, shouting, "You can't go through there, don't you see it's forbidden?"

The horses were no longer responding to the reins, the smaller children were crying, buried in the straw. They passed several large posters with a difficult word, SESQUICENTEN-NIAL, which they couldn't read, and Belisaria began to cry silently because this was hell and she had to pray to the Little Virgin to get them away from there.

Finally, they found a street that led them away from the

· *Open Door*

plaza, although they had to force their way through the crowd. They passed before a whitewashed house that was at the center of the commotion, with its two windows covered by green grates at either side of the door.

"Look, a door almost as pretty as ours!" shouted one of the children, but nothing could get their attention, not even that flare of lights and the contours of the cathedral that hung in the night like an admonition. In the sky, evil fires were exploding, red and green, and in the brightness their faces seemed to be those of souls in pain.

Like a lost soul, the cart was being dragged through that cyclone of shouts and colors, through the pitching and rolling of the city.

The guns thundered again, the clamor was deafening, and as soon as the horses found themselves in a street free of the encircling hordes of people, they burst into a gallop.

Orosmán couldn't get the horses under control until they reached the open country, where the city was no more than a red stain in the sky, like a sunset. From then on the long, tiring journey went slower, but it never halted. Finally they arrived at the two crossed posts that stood over the place where the hut had been. The cold was crouched there, as if waiting for them. The need for a fire was great, especially after that long hard trip that had lasted a night, a day, and part of another night. A fire was also needed to scare off the souls of the dead, and one of the children groaned, "Burn the door." He had been trying to light some twigs, but got hardly a spark.

"Not the door, no!" Belisaria protested. "It's the only thing we have, it watches over us. If we burn it, for sure a curse will fall on us."

The silence was long and painful.

"A worse curse would be for Grandmother to die of cold," Orosmán concluded.

They took leave of the door with piety and devotion, but the flames grew rapidly, and the devils' faces twisted into grimaces that mocked them, all of them, including the angel.

But they did have the heat, and when Don Zoilo passed by in the morning, the coals were still burning. He was enormously surprised to find that Orosmán, with his wife, his mother, and his children, had returned, and that all were praying at the foot of the wooden cross, the only sign of the hut that remained.

"How come you're back?" he asked them without dismounting. "You're going to have to begin again."

"Yes," Orosmán answered. "And now we don't even have the door to protect us. But we had to return, even though we may die of cold."

And looking at his hands, he added, "Because when we arrived there, Tucumán was at war."

tr. Hortense Carpentier and J. Jorge Castello

· *Open Door*

City

of the

Unknown

to Juan Goyanarte

When I first heard him sing, I told myself, This man has a voice that could raise the dead. And for once I knew words wouldn't fail me.

My life doesn't have much to do with fantasy, not even science fiction. It's made of little things that the gods offer me when I am deserving and which I recognize as different from a million other things. Take pebbles, for example. I know that pebbles are my friends. One day when I was feeling especially clearheaded, I found a pebble shaped like a hen. A while later, I found one that was like a woman with only one breast and a hole for a navel. Unimportant things, of course, compared with my city. I first discovered the city in my dreams; later I looked for it where I had dreamed it, on the other side of the Andes, overlooking the Pacific. It's a city of pointed arches and hard red walls that I thought the mountains had created for me.

He has a voice that could raise the dead, I kept telling myself as I listened to him sing. I knew that, in order to reach him, I had to descend many steps, the same steps as those I descended when I was moved by a dark purpose, like the force that had driven me to that neighborhood of longshoremen and sly prostitutes.

I didn't like looking for him, knowing of his existence, unmasking him. His was the voice of another race, torn from his guts after the third glass of brandy, and only I knew it, although there were other people there, pale and ghostly next to his black animal skin, who listened in an almost reverent silence. I returned twice, three times, always at the fifth stroke of twelve, as he began to sing. I came in time to witness the ritual of patrons putting aside cards and dice and licking their lips in anticipation of his singing. On the third day I decided: I will take him to my city that overhangs the sea. His voice could raise the dead, and my city is full of spirits that dance around me and tell me things each time I arrive from across the mountains.

Only he could raise the dead of my city and enable me to understand that contour of nature which, helped by the wind, imitates the work of men. Those who died there already knew the mystery that hung from the highest peaks, the mystery that kept me awake those lonely nights among the rocks. Year after year, every summer, almost religiously, I'd leave the volcanoes of Copahue to try and solve the secret of my city. Seated at the table in the corner, listening to him sing, I realized that I couldn't do anything without his help.

Why should I let daylight rub out his existence, I thought. And the following morning I returned to the seedy club to ask where I could find him. But there he was, in the same spot as the night before, only with a changed expression. His empty bottle rolled across the floor. Cautiously, I went down the steps and brought a chair to his table. I tried to explain. I talked for

· Open Door

an hour, and I didn't succeed in getting so much as a glance from him.

"No one can help but you," I pleaded. "I'm leaving in two weeks. Come with me." All my pleading, and still he didn't lift his eyes, so I left, dragging my feet in despair. As I went out to the street, it occurred to me that perhaps he didn't understand ordinary words and that he could only be reached through some obscure, cabalistic signals. I ran back to see if something could still be done, and I pushed open the swinging door. He looked up, his eyes showing a flicker of understanding, enough to feed my determination. Night after night I got there just as he was beginning to sing. Gradually, I moved out of my corner and into the sad light that encircled him, but he gave no sign of recognition.

The night before my departure I decided to play my last card. I sat at the table in front of him, put my knapsack on the floor beside me, and waited. He seemed asleep. Only when he began to sing did his eyes brighten up.

I need him to revive my dead so I can understand, I kept repeating to myself for strength. Finally, I took the tickets to Copahue out of my pocket and put them right before his eyes. He looked down and stopped his song abruptly. His silence stirred the quiet. The audience recovered its composure. A man drew his chair close to mine and tried to embrace me. But I only had eyes for the singer. I could see his muscles tense up until his arm shot out like a spring and hit the man's jaw. The man fell, dragging the chair down with him. My singer picked up the tickets and the knapsack with one hand and with the other pushed me across the room and up the stairs.

In the miserable hotel at El Bajo, I discovered that his body had the exact shape I wished for, but he didn't want to have anything to do with mine. Or with my gratitude. The next morning our clumsy trip began, along dusty pampa roads, along mountain paths, nights and days with interminable delays. He traveled silent and erect, seeing nothing, never complaining or showing surprise. He needs liquor, I thought. I'll buy him a few bottles so he'll sing with all his might when we arrive at my city.

As daylight was fading, we arrived at Copahue, the valley of volcanoes, with its hot springs from the bowels of the earth that turned the mountain into hell. We arrived to the smell of sulphur and the sight of eternal snows.

In the hotel it was our custom to sleep in the same bed but not to touch each other. However, that night the temperature fell below zero and he began to shiver under the blankets. I didn't want him to suffer next to me, and almost instinctively I gave him a little of my warmth. Suddenly his arm came alive, each cell in his body came alive, and there was nothing I could do but remain as I was and let the rites be fulfilled.

I woke up late that morning and wanted to feel him close. I reached out across the covers, but I didn't find him. I felt that he had left me forever. Intentions and laws had been violated by an offense to purity, by a yielding to desire, just as we were approaching my city. I dressed as quickly as I could and ran out, heedlessly bucking the wind that pushed me back and made me fall, impervious to the tiny mounds of lava that spurted in my path, burning my feet. The farther I ran, the more he faded from my mind, his arms, his black body. "My dead souls," I screamed, "I am losing my dead."

I was sure I would never see him again, that he had vanished like my breath. But at last I saw him by a lagoon of boiling mud. He was looking at the giant bubbles that swelled and ruptured in deafening bursts. He was cold and shivering, and he seemed mesmerized.

I seized him by the hand like a child and took him across to the other side of the valley, to the Indian market. I bought him a thick poncho, and I laughed to see him so solemn, looking so much like a gaucho. He smiled, and suddenly his face took on the same expression he had when he sang.

We bought food, we hired horses for the following morning, we raced from place to place, hand in hand, arranging the details of our great adventure. I didn't forget the brandy either, but as I was paying for it, I realized I wouldn't have enough money left for the return trip. But at that moment the return trip was unimportant.

At the break of dawn, we left the stone houses and the muddy, red-hot lagoons behind us. We let ourselves be carried through the barren mountain paths, through roads hanging over precipices, onto narrow tree trunks lying across turbulent streams. Only the horses knew the secret of how not to topple over the edge, and they had to be allowed to move ahead unbridled.

At Chanchoco, a small Chilean village of flat-roofed huts and silent Indians, we broke our long journey. But we couldn't rest in that sea of hostile glances. We stayed there only long enough to eat something hot and change horses; then we were on our way again, through the mountains, toward my city, to bring my dead back to life.

Up there in the mountains, where the landscape is dreary and oppressive, there is a feeling of light-headedness, but he felt cold and shook under his poncho. I was beginning to feel sorry that I had brought this man, accustomed to heat and languor, to this climate. But the prospect of unveiling the mystery of my city made me cruel, and I kept moving ahead without looking at him. Every so often I would hand him the bottle, and after a long swig he would seem to revive. In that way we finally reached the large rock corral where I always let the horses free.

We climbed the rugged mountain on foot. He must have known intuitively that we were close, for he began to sing in a low voice, breathless, until at last we reached the caves and high walls of bright earth colors that formed my city over the sea. As always, I was overcome by the strange peace of the place, and I sat next to him on the edge of the precipice, our backs to the waters roaring below. I had to restrain myself to keep from running through the labyrinths, and I remained quiet while he contemplated my city, as if to penetrate its meaning.

He began to sing again, his voice vibrating against the rocks. While the sun was sinking behind the mountains, his song lofted and swelled, invading the dark reaches of the caves. I tried hard not to hear his voice; I wanted to get the message that would come from the dead. His song entered the tunnels, whirled around, and echoed back changed. Suddenly, where the whirlwind should have been, I saw a ghostly light that rose from the earth, a wavering white vapor. In that strange light the mystery would be unraveled, and I held my breath in order not to frighten it away.

I didn't want to look at him, but I prayed for him not to stop singing, because his song would bring me the truth. He kept on singing, louder, deeper, and the ghostly light assumed the shapes that were separating out from the shadows, striving to reach the light of the violet-colored sunset.

At first the shapes seemed nebulous, but then, little by little, they grew more defined, until my expectation turned into terror and I wanted to scream. But I couldn't. I wanted to draw back. But I couldn't. The forms were in front of me, closing in. I expected their souls, but their bodies appeared before me instead, bones with flesh hanging from them, sinister smiles without lips.

"Shut up!" I screamed at him when I recovered my voice, but he didn't hear me and he continued singing while the dead came closer, implacable, swaying to the twisting rhythm of his song.

"Be quiet, be quiet!"

· *Open Door*

In desperation I covered my eyes, but nothing could stop the forms, and the images slipped through my fingers as they advanced. Only he had the power to make them disappear, if he would stop singing, but he intended to go on. One push would silence him eternally. There was no other choice, and it was so simple. The rocks under him gave way, and he fell into the abyss without a whimper.

The corpses had been snuffed out with the last note of his song. It took me a long time to get over the visceral sensation of horror and loathing they produced in me. But then I realized how alone I was in the night and in the world, and I began to feel all the pain that had been his, the breaking of his dark body. At some time that dark body will soar back up into the mountains—that is, if someone like him, with a voice capable of raising the dead, comes to my city.

I am still waiting.

tr. Hortense Carpentier and J. Jorge Castello

Nihil

Obstat

As you might suppose, I'm seeking total absolution of my sins. That's not something new. No, it's been that way with me since I was a boy, since I was eleven and robbed a cap full of coins from a blind beggar. I did it so I could buy myself a medal, and of course I had figured things out very carefully: the medal had the Sacred Heart on one side, and on the other an inscription offering nine hundred days of indulgence to anyone who said an Our Father before the image. If my calculations were right, four Our Fathers were enough to get Heaven to forgive me for the theft. The time left over figured to be clear profit: nine hundred days in itself isn't an eternity, but a series of nine hundred days, one after another, adds up to a holiday in Paradise. Now, that's a pleasure worth contemplating.

As for having a good time after death—don't tell me it's a joke to have to walk through this God's earth burdened with gnawing sins and guilt hanging over you, weighing you down if they can be absolved so easily.

· *Open Door*

Also, I thought about the wafers, which were terrific while they lasted. Let me tell you that I, Juan Lucas, named after two evangelists, as is proper, attended Mass at six o'clock every morning to take Communion. By making a little effort to behave myself, more or less, and by going to a different church each time, I could make one confession last me all week. Seven days of getting up at dawn left me with a crop of six sacred wafers that I could keep in reserve against hard times. I stored them in a carved wooden box on which I had pasted an image of Saint Inez and which I purified with holy water from one of the several bottles I keep around. The most critical moment came when I had to slip the wafer out of my mouth after Communion, but if I settled in the darkest corner in the church, it was easy. Even the pious old women were half asleep at that hour. They didn't realize that, a few feet away, they had a saint, and that I was that saint, denying myself the responsibility for even the least offensive of my most delicious sins.

Generally, my stock of sacred wafers was used up during summer vacation, what with the temptation at the beaches with girls in bathing suits and the wafers I sold to friends who wanted to redeem themselves once and for all. As you can see, I've spread the light among my friends, even though some of them may not have deserved it.

My self-Communion was a simple, but devout, ceremony. At night, after a wild spree, I would bless the wafer again and administer it to myself, celebrating my own purity. It was the perfect absolution, without all the church rigmarole that makes you lose so many good hours at the beach. Besides, going to sleep with a bad conscience upset me a lot, as if I hadn't brushed my teeth. You know what I mean?

Last year I met Matías. Frankly, I'm a healthy, happy boy, as you can see, at peace with the Creator at all times. Matías, on the other hand, is a tragic one: gloomy, always dressed in black, always frowning. At first I thought maybe that kind of behavior led to salvation, and I began to imitate him; I dressed in black and I stopped laughing. At night we walked the dark streets and he would talk to me.

"The path to God is for the chosen. Torturing yourself won't amount to anything if you're not one of us. Kneel down, you despicable worm, and pray."

My manner of praying, of kneeling, and of being a despicable worm persuaded him that I was indeed one of them.

"Tomorrow the grand penitence begins," he said to me one day. "We will fast for three days, we will live only on bread and water, in absolute silence and in deepest darkness."

The whole thing was beginning to look ugly to me, but I took heart and asked him, "How many days of indulgence do you think you'll earn with all that sacrifice?"

"You're a worm, no doubt about it. I knew it. A perfect mercenary, selfish. And to make matters worse, you're not seeking the benefits of this world, but of the other, which is more serious. You know how God punished the greedy and the arrogant."

He stared at me with loathing for a long time, and then added, "But I will save your soul. Save it simply for your own good, and not to find my salvation in you, as you would do in my place."

He rolled up the sleeves of the habit he wore when he was sure he wouldn't be seen by anyone who knew him as a bank clerk, and he shouted, "I'm going to tear that lust out of you for all eternity, even if it means ripping your skin to shreds!"

He grabbed the whip he had hanging in what he called his "gaucho corner" and began to lash me furiously. I suppose he did it for my own good, as he said, but I assure you I was happy he hadn't decided to use spurs or a branding iron instead. My back turned all purple, but he didn't stop until his arm grew tired. I can't see why my penitence has to be in direct ratio with the endurance of his biceps. It's unfair: there are days when he

· *Open Door*

isn't so strict and I scarcely have to atone for anything. And the blows, as you can well imagine, don't add up like wafers.

The fasting? Oh, yes, of course we did that. As far as the darkness was concerned, it was deep and total only from dusk to dawn, from the time the bright neon signs outside the window were turned off until the first rays of sunlight filtered through the blinds. You know how these modern apartments are, everything comes in: noise, smells, lights. The flashing reds and greens from the neon sign gave Matías a devil's face that puffed up and shrank as he ate the dry bread. Personally, I wasn't too excited; I don't believe that's any way to achieve saintliness. I prefer simpler things. Deeper. Blessed things. At least with the whippings there was pain, and I could believe something was happening. But not eating, and sitting in the dark, and hardly speaking. That can't redeem anyone. It's too boring.

"We have to sleep in one cot to make sure we suffer from discomfort even in our sleep," said Matías.

In reply, I suggested that we sleep on the floor. "It's hard and very uncomfortable and at least we won't have to squeeze together in this heat."

"No. We must be up against each other, pressed tightly together so our vital force doesn't escape us. We must unite our souls. We must conserve the spirit that eludes us so easily when it is weak. Embrace me, brother."

As far as I'm concerned, no one will ever get me with that story again. Matías did what he could, of course, even to the point where he wanted to kiss me on the mouth to infuse a little of his saintliness into me. It didn't do anything for me, though, all that sacrificing on his part. In the book where I keep an account of the pardon time earned, I could only record three years, one for each day we spent penned up together. And, as you know, three years of Paradise in the sum of eternity isn't very much.

It was at that time that Adela came along, a splendid girl but very earthy, very different from Matías. She never wanted to go to Mass with me, not even to confession. I tried to persuade her to swallow one of my wafers, but she laughed at me. She came to my house often, stayed a little while, and *whack!* we would commit the sin of the flesh. She had soft skin. And it was warm, always warm and vibrant. I tried to explain it to Matías: I told him that when I had her in my bed, so blonde, such clear eyes, I imagined she was an angel. Nevertheless, Matías answered: "An angel? She's a devil! You must leave this woman who is Satan incarnate, this serpent who puts the apple in your hands and will not stop until she sees you dragging yourself through every hell."

"No," I said, defending her. "Adela is a good girl. You can't talk that way about her. She doesn't hurt anyone, and she makes me happy."

"Lust!" he roared, until at last I realized that he was right. But I can't do anything else, even though at times I think it's wrong. It seems most wrong when Adela comes to knock at Matías's door and calls after me like a lunatic. At those times, Matías fiercely defends me; he throws her out, clawing at her, and then comes into the bedroom to quiet me and to tell me not to worry.

But I'm troubled, Father, and that's why I want you to tell me: how much time in Paradise can I add in the book for having given up Adela so much against my wishes?

tr. Hortense Carpentier and J. Jorge Castello

· *Open Door*

A Family

for

Clotilde

Rolo spent that morning, like so many others, watching Rolando. For his father, taking a rest meant exhausting himself physically: long jogs down the deserted beach, racing, leaping, one exercise after another. He was forty-six and still physically fit. Rolo was about to turn seventeen; it was a serious age, and unlike his father, he felt sick and tired of the world.

Standing at the top of a dune, or drinking an orangeade, Rolo watched the sun glistening on his father's golden back as he conscientiously did his calisthenics. Rolando was a good athlete and he knew it. Rolo looked at his own pale body, narrow at the shoulders, and understood why he was ashamed to walk next to his father when they were both in bathing suits. Even so, as the season progressed, and they rented a cabana, Rolo preferred going to the beach with his father to sitting in a beach chair next to his mother all day long. She was unusually emphatic in her attitudes, and if in November and December she was busy in the house and didn't take a moment's rest, for the remainder of the vacation she would forget the house and family and dedicate herself entirely to sunbathing. She wanted to return to Buenos Aires looking as if she had had a good time.

That afternoon there was nothing to do, as usual, and Rolo sat on the fence and dreamed about dancing, about girls in bikinis, about friends he missed. At four o'clock Don Luis clambered up from the beach along the path between the dunes that led to Rolando's house. Don Luis's cart was massive, and corroded by the sea.

"Good afternoon," said the driver.

"Hi," said Rolo.

"You could make that sound more cheerful. I have the valises of the lady who's going to stay in the cottage in back of your house. Your family's lucky, I told your father, because at this time of year nobody rents or sells."

The horses pulling the cart rested after the hard trek. Only the pony was impatient and breathing hard.

"Uh huh," Rolo mumbled without enthusiasm, but he looked intently at the white leather bags and the enormous old-fashioned trunk.

"Looks like the lady's going to stay a long time, eh?"

"Uh huh."

"All summer?"

"All summer, part of autumn, the rest of her life. That goes for us, too; we'll never move away from here. Buried."

He dug his penknife into the trunk of a pine tree. He wanted to go away, anyplace. If only Pinamar were a port, then he could at least imagine trips. . . .

It was Sunday morning. With his jacket over his shoulder, Rolo walked through the trees surrounding the house, along the border of thickly clustered acacias, to the garden of the rear cottage. He had forgotten about the new tenant, but there she was to remind him, reclining on a deck chair in the shade,

· *Open Door*

showing a great deal of white flesh and gleaming red hair. Rolo stopped short.

"Hi, darling. Where're you off to?" She had a warm, soft voice.

"To Mass," he answered grudgingly.

"To Mass?" Coming from her, the word sounded new and mysterious.

The sun was burning bright. Rolo wanted to stretch out in the cool air under the pines and simply listen to her. Instead he said, "Yes, to Mass. You may think our chapel small and ugly and unfinished, but that's not what counts if you want to go to Mass."

"Hmm. And if you were to stay here at my side and sip a gin and tonic, wouldn't that be nicer than going to church?"

"No."

"Well, your good father would prefer to sit here with me. He isn't like you. He doesn't go to Mass. Yesterday afternoon he passed by here on horseback five times. Just a little while ago I saw him in a bathing suit; he must be off for a swim. . . . Stay a bit."

She had deep-set dark-gray eyes. Rolo ran off without answering her.

I'll show that wild woman I'm not like my father, he thought. Who does the old man think he is, coming through here all hot and excited? I'll teach them. . . .

As the days passed, Rolando grew pensive. Rolo followed him all over the house, taunting him whenever he could. But Rolando didn't complain; in fact, it was practically impossible to drag a word out of him on any subject.

"Dear, don't put your feet on the sofa, you'll dirty the cretonne."

"Dear, move a little so I can open the windows and air the place a bit."

And the dear did as he was asked, without protest. Astonishing.

Rolo first became suspicious when he noticed that his father no longer got up at seven o'clock to take his early-morning swim. Then, one afternoon during siesta, he saw Rolando sneaking out through the kitchen door. Rolo raced upstairs to the attic and peered out of the small window just as Rolando entered Clotilde's house—without knocking, as if she were one of the family.

They're going to find out what I can do, and they'll have to learn the hard way, Rolo thought. They'll see. No one plays dirty with me. I was invited first.

Rolo had never thought of himself as patient, but sometimes virtues surface in time of need. Squatting on the dry, brittle leaves behind the bank of acacias, he waited two long hours for Rolando to abandon her body, the body that must be so white between the sheets, so soft to sink one's hands into. He thought of the other poor bodies he had known, withered and worn, smelling of his friends who had been there before him.

Clotilde must be different, he thought, and he had her in the palm of his hand. Now that he knew their secret and could denounce them. Soon he would show those two he also was a man. Rolo, little Rolo, would follow his father's footsteps to Clotilde's flesh. He would put his mouth where his father's had been, he would carefully imitate each of his gestures. The wait was long and torturous, but the compensation of Clotilde's hot, slippery body would come.

A blossoming azalea exuded a subtle smell that Rolo was not prepared to appreciate. Beyond the flowers, beyond the walls of the house, he imagined his naked father on the white Clotilde, and he knew his turn would come.

Rolando wouldn't take long. The door with the slightly flaky green paint would open just wide enough for him to slip out, and Rolo would only wait long enough to see Rolando recede in the distance. Then he would enter quickly and take Clotilde by force. She'd have no way to defend herself.

That wasn't how it happened at all, of course. Clotilde saw

him, called to him, and he surrendered as meekly as a puppy. It was Clotilde who guided his hands along the trail of his father's hands.

"He asked me to swear not to say anything to you, and I swore and asked him to go on kissing me. . . . As if I cared . . ."

Rolando laughed a cold, empty laugh, but Clotilde went on chattering. When she tried to cuddle up against his body, however, the muscles of his back arched one by one, and he leaped up, smashing his fist on the night table. A little while later, though, he sauntered into the bathroom as if nothing had happened. He came back looking calm and lay down beside her, but then doubt assailed him again and he shook Clotilde violently, shouting, "I'm better than the kid, right? Tell me I'm better than the kid!"

"Yes, yes," she said, and she thought of the boy who had never dared to sigh, and she felt tender toward him.

The following afternoon, Rolando told his wife that he was going out to get some cigarettes, and she seemed to believe him.

Rolo, however, couldn't say, "I'm going out to get some cigarettes," because he wasn't allowed to smoke. But he was allowed to come and go as he pleased, so he didn't have to make up excuses in order to visit Clotilde and engage in something far more serious than smoking.

As soon as his father left, Rolo, as usual, ran upstairs to spy on him from the attic window. The scene was always the same: Rolando, hurrying, furtive, ran into her open arms, and he, Rolo, felt happy because he would soon be on the path his father had paved for him, thus proving that he was no less a man.

But any man is a man, given certain attributes. In a sense, Clotilde was as much a man as either of them: she manipulated them as she pleased, frustrating them, pitting one against the other, favoring one over the other. She was the real man there, and she knew it. She reaffirmed it every night in the bed that often bore the weight and heat of one of them before the weight and heat of the other had faded. Clotilde. She would look at herself in the mirror, caressing her full breasts, smiling and showing her teeth, white, even, indifferent. Thinking was a tremendous effort for her: she simply felt happy and at times nostalgic. She also enjoyed tantalizing those who had the good fortune to touch her. And she felt no remorse about it.

In the big house on the other side of the dense acacias and the soft rosy mattress of pine needles, Estela, Rolo's mother and Rolando's wife, was also in the habit of looking at herself in the bathroom mirror. Her image emerged from the cloud of foam she used to clean the mirror. She ran the rag back and forth furiously, sometimes allowing only her eyes to appear, sometimes an ear or a corner of her mouth that revealed a hurt expression. She would have loved to rub that image out altogether, but there it was, facing her, inexorable, and all she could do was wash the mirror and hope a little of the cleanliness would rub off on her soul.

She knew it: her two men were gone forever, gone to the other woman because Estela was soft and easy, not hard and strong like the other one.

Rolo crouched behind the thick maze of acacias. He knew that the door would open at any moment, and he curled up even more in his hiding place. But it was a false alarm, or, more accurately, a false hope. His father was lingering longer than usual on Clotilde's body; it wasn't fair; Rolo was restless. What if she was detaining him? Could she have asked his father not to leave her? Still, the one time he had asked her how Rolando caressed her, she had answered, "Not exactly out of this world . . ."

"Please tell me what he does with you. I don't want to be less of a man."

"No, I like the differences. He's a brute. He beats me. Sometimes he slaps me across the face and shouts while he's making love to me."

· *Open Door*

She had turned toward him and put his uncombed head on her belly. "But you are soft, almost like a girl. I like to stroke your face, your shoulders, your back."

"Have you ever done it with a woman?"

"Hmm," she had answered vaguely. Sometimes he interpreted the *hmm* as yes, sometimes as no, depending on his mood.

He had been hiding behind the acacias for over two hours. Soon his mother would wake up from her siesta; he was furious. Clotilde knew very well that he was there, but there wasn't even a sign from her. That whore. Worse than a whore, devouring anything that came her way—men, women, old people, children; a sexual ostrich.

To calm himself, Rolo walked behind the cottage. Hidden behind the shutters, the father watched his son's every move.

He doesn't know yet Clotilde isn't here. What the hell, let him suffer. I'm suffering too, Rolando kept repeating to himself.

Rolo stopped abruptly. Behind the climbing jasmines, in front of the bedroom window, there was a mound of cigar butts, some crushed, some smoked down to a nub, some only half-smoked, all with a cork tip. His father had been there many times, probably hoping his son would leave Clotilde's bed once and for all so he, Rolando, could go back to her and have the last laugh.

Rolando knew his secret, he knew his son had also been there, just as he had been before him, just as he would be again. Always Rolando had to have the last word, the last loud laugh, the last act of love. His father always bested him, always flattened him out. It was Clotilde's fault this time for telling him everything, for not keeping her mouth shut. Whore.

Behind the shutters, Rolando felt jealous of his son and happy to see him standing there confused. Clotilde had left him a note saying she would be gone until evening. She must be avoiding him; she knew he would be coming that afternoon.

And that poor boy, standing there disconsolate, believing his father was performing heaven-knows-what feats, not realizing that those feats are usually a young man's prerogative.

On either side of the closed shutters, father and son stood overcome, defeated. He'll stay in there all afternoon, Rolo thought, all night, forcing her to forget about me. Finally Rolo decided to leave. He walked slowly down the path, kicking pebbles and telling himself that, after all, Clotilde must prefer women anyway, the struggle wasn't worth it.

Rolando watched Rolo move in the distance. He may be too thin, thought Rolando, and his back may curve, but still and all, Rolo is young and strong and intense in the way women like.

Neither of them could guess that Clotilde was fed up with the whole affair, with Rolo hiding in the garden while Rolando was with her, and then Rolando pacing back and forth in the garden like a caged lion, although he would never admit it. As if she didn't know that they were searching for each other through her.

That night Rolo helped his mother wash the dishes, a thing he seldom did.

"Mama," he said after a long silence, "do you know the woman who rents the cottage in the back?"

"No."

There was an uncomfortable pause.

"You should get to know her. Make friends with her. She's very nice."

"I don't need friends. Not the likes of her, anyway."

"Why not make friends with her, Mama? After all, she's our tenant." It was a bold statement to make to a mother who must have known quite well what was going on. "You could go see her tomorrow and bring her a piece of that delicious cake you make. . . ."

His mother wiped the burners of the stove furiously, then took off her apron and went into the bedroom.

· *Open Door*

Rolando was in bed. He had not gone for a walk in the woods, he was not reading in the living room. He was simply there, installed in bed as if he'd been waiting for her.

She spent a long time in the bathroom and came back into the bedroom in her nightgown.

"Estela," Rolando said, "Estela, you've been alone so much, too much lately. If we're going to stay here another two months, why not get to know people?"

"My friends are coming after Epiphany. . . ."

"That's a month away, Estela. Meanwhile what? Stay shut up in this house? The weather's nice now for the beach. You ought to have a friend to go with you."

"You have someone in mind?"

"In mind, no . . . the tenant, maybe. She seems pleasant enough."

It must be a conspiracy, she thought. They must be making fun of me. She was sick and tired of being treated like an idiot for trying to keep peace in the family. They wanted to see her act, well, she would act. The fight's on, she thought; let's see who wins. An inspection of the enemy camp can't hurt; that will give me an equal chance.

"Fine," she said, gently as usual. "If tomorrow's all right with you, I'll go visit her and bring some cake for tea."

Rolando was astonished at the ease with which he had convinced her.

The men in the family are sadder than ever. While they were enjoying themselves they could afford to overlook her pain. It had been a clean fight between men, altogether understandable. They had eaten with gusto, shown their happiness in an effort to make each other suffer. They had paid no attention to the woman who sat in front of them, doing her best not to burst into tears.

Now the situation is very different. Estela is exultant, she has turned into an eloquent conversationalist. She has acquired a new grandeur. She, Estela, now occupies an ample and warm place where the two men had once fit. Now Estela is alone and triumphant in Clotilde's bosom.

Listless, they never look at her or at each other. They only walk back and forth in the house that is no longer a home because Estela has neglected the floor, the meals. And she no longer bothers to put flowers on the table. She has other interests. From the last bite of lunch until sunset, she spends the day in Clotilde's cottage. A lightning friendship, one might say, blissful love at first sight, the reunion of queen bees, with the drones buzzing around like lost souls. Sometimes they circle around Estela, trying to get her back; at other times they attempt to get back to Clotilde. They haven't succeeded with either—no bread and no cake.

Finally, they are ready for a confrontation. But what can those two dispossessed beings say to each other, those two males who have learned that the only way they can reach each other is through silent competition?

The days go on until Rolo can't stand it any longer. He walks over to his old hiding place to spy on the cottage. He has hoped to set his mother against his father, but the wind has blown another way: good-by, Clotilde; good-by, love; good-by. Estela now takes up all her time, all her gestures, all her words. She has shown herself to be the most astute: she has conquered Clotilde effortlessly. "You have a formidable mother," Clotilde says to him the one time he sees her alone. And she doesn't say another word—no apologies, no gratitude for what had gone on before. About-face, march, and once again she is inside her cottage with the door firmly closed.

Huddled behind the acacias, Rolo is remembering the past with Clotilde. He knows that a few feet away Rolando is taking his customary walk behind the climbing jasmines. Both are caught in the same trap, spying on the women who are devoted to one another and have no intention of parting.

· *Open Door*

Neither knows what he is waiting for, and each ignores the other's presence. They ignore everything except the world from which they have been excluded forever. They listen, and each in his hiding place receives on his face the lash of a kind of laugh, a submissive laugh, somewhat ashamed, that rises suddenly to cover up something and then lowers in tone, changing into a whisper that filters into the bones. Rolo leaps up and runs toward the bedroom window and, unexpectedly, collides with his father, who has also left his hiding place on hearing that laugh that threatens not to end. They look at each other accusingly, but neither says a word. They are both outside forever, and it is only because they had had the idea of putting Estela inside the cottage. Now Estela was never going to leave, for she had awakened Clotilde's laugh.

It is a well-tuned murmuring, like the pines, caressing, loving. Suddenly it begins to rain, softly at first, then with some fury. They remain in the garden, drenched, waiting until night falls.

Inside the cottage, Estela doesn't feel the cold, the rain, the night. She smiles with beatific happiness because her plan has succeeded. She makes Clotilde repeat once again the Act of Contrition and the Prayer to the Virgin. "Hail Mary, full of grace . . ." The prayer returns and undulates like a laugh that leaves Clotilde's contrite lips. And Estela, who doesn't really care about Clotilde's contrition, smiles because she knows that she has won back her men.

tr. Hortense Carpentier and J. Jorge Castello

Trial

of the

Virgin

to Arturo Cuadrado

"Very pretty and all that, but what has She done for us? Not even a minor miracle. We're fed up, I tell you."

Over his head hung a bloated starfish, its eyes staring out from a tangle of net. His face was ravaged by wind and salt, his hands shapeless from years of tugging at nets.

"A dog's life, I tell you. And that *Temerario* sinking at the entrance to the harbor. We could practically see them drowning, but we couldn't do a thing about it. Of course, it was the boss's fault that Luque went out again. With a storm like that, you can't go out, the *Siempre Lista* crew told him. But Luque wasn't one to lose a good catch of salmon when he'd found it. He thought he was in Her good graces. He kept a picture of the Virgin alongside the helm. But Virgin of Miracles or no Virgin of Miracles, I personally don't think She ever heard Luque.

"She had been brought from Spain, a gift of fishermen of other seas. A pretty statuette, a little sad, with layers of lace that looked like foam. A pretty statuette, and better still, miraculous; anyway, that's what they said. That's why She never lacked a carefully lighted candle, or two, or three. At Her feet She had votive candles in tin cans, more to tempt Her to grant wishes than in gratitude for some cure She hadn't performed—a little like those plaster eggs left in nests to encourage hens to lay more eggs. But this, clearly, wasn't a miracle-laying statuette, although those who brought Her swear to the contrary, and you can't ignore that kind of faith."

At first, the fishermen thought the image would have to be allowed to get used to the place. Ironically, some said that She should be tempted with better bait, but fishermen shook their heads: the ways of Heaven had nothing to do with the secrets of good fishing.

While they prepared hooks on the long line to catch salmon, or mended the seines, they never stopped thinking of Her, hoping for some miracle. When they returned, their ships loaded to the gunnels, they knew very well that their catch was no miracle at all, but a fulfillment of the law of the sea, in effect long before She had appeared in the village. On the dock, as they flung the salmon through the air onto the truck, they thought to themselves: A true miracle would be finding a good concrete dock under our feet one morning instead of those rotting boards, where any one of us could break a leg on a moonless night.

The women had a more fanciful, although no less selfish, idea of the Virgin's obligations. When the boats were out of port, they gathered around Her, more to envy her fine velvet cloak, the lace trim, and the silver necklaces than to pray for the safe return of their men.

Galloping across the vast desert, the wind came to the melancholy little town and found it empty, the men on the high seas and the women in church: work and faith, the perfect combination to let the wind run unchecked toward the beach and whirl about wildly and play with María, who found it pleasing to amuse herself with the wind, to let it pass between her legs or tangle in her hair or tickle her skin, making her laugh.

"Look at that mad creature, making a fool of herself. She's too old to spend her days collecting shells and running around barefoot."

María never looked enviously at the Virgin's silver necklaces, because she had a long necklace of her own, of snail shells. She never went to church either, and she ignored the women who tried to turn the Virgin against her with stories of María as a new Eve sent to seduce their men or, even worse, a venomous serpent with the body of a woman, ready to spring on the village and cause sin to flow through the village like rich wine. But why would that matter if the women were the beneficiaries of this sin, and if it was their virtue that slipped away through their husbands' splendid nets? Free on the beach, María was the threat that someday would break the long-established order, leaving them out in the cold.

"Little Virgin, saintly figure, give me blue cloth so I can make myself a new dress. Or María will take my Ramón away."

"Oh, Little Virgin, to think that she carries your name! She is the devil itself! Yesterday I saw my husband looking at her. His eyes were shining as they have never shone for me. She has bewitched him!"

The Virgin had a face that seemed to understand everything. And yet, month after month, María continued to run, free and wild, and so did the desire of the men. But why should María want men, when the caresses of the wind were so much softer and asked nothing of her?

As they drank their wine in the café across from the wharfs, the fishermen didn't look at the mouth of the river or keep vigil for the high tide that would permit them to go out. Their eyes were fixed on the spot where, sooner or later, María would pass by, her hair tangled with seaweed.

· *Open Door*

One day the summer came at last, the sun appeared, the sea paused to take a breath, and the cold wasteland beyond the houses glistened with unexpected tones. The fishermen did not leave port, they stayed in the café, their glasses before them, waiting to see María pass by. The air shimmered, radiant, an omen of important events. As the sun was setting, herding a flock of rosy clouds, María appeared. Her soaked dress outlined her body: she had made friends with the sea in defiance of the wind that had abandoned her. Many pairs of eyes followed her as she walked home, many potential friends who thought they could give her more satisfaction than the wind or the sea. It was a moment of silence, of muted sighs, of unuttered calls. Then they continued drinking as if nothing had happened, and went home with the desire for María pounding in their hearts.

Felipe, who was recently married, found the only flower in the village where it grew, hidden between some rotted boards a few feet from his house. He plucked it for his wife but, after careful thought, turned around and went to church to place it at the feet of the Virgin.

"I bring you the only wild flower that has grown in this port. I have never asked you for anything, but now I want María. Give me María, just this once, and I will bring you flowers from the most distant corners."

Felipe was not the only one that night to have the brilliant idea of asking the Virgin for help in getting the virgin. Among the others was Hernán Cavarrubias, carrying his heavy bronze lantern, his treasured possession, under his right arm (his left having been torn off by a winch) to give to the Virgin when he asked Her to make María his. After all, he argued, if we're dealing in miracles, there is no reason a one-armed man should have less luck with a woman than a whole man.

The following morning, the boats left at dawn, filled with hope. When they reached the sandbar, the point of real danger, the fishermen neglected their helms and gazed back at the beach, where the sun had risen and María was bathing naked.

The women went to church a little later that day, carrying gifts along with fervent prayers for the Virgin of Miracles. But they found the altar already covered with offerings. At first they felt hatred and jealousy. The Virgin was monopolizing the generosity of their men. But it didn't take long for them to understand that it couldn't be a mere statue that the men loved so much. The shells, the flower, the ring, and even Hernán Cavarrubias's lantern represented something more: the smell of a female.

They held a long secret meeting in the church, and decided to consult old Raquel and bring her the gifts intended for the Virgin: the old woman was a famous witch, and she could be impartial, for she had no man to lose.

Old Raquel well knew the depths of the human soul. "That woman has addled their brains because she's out of reach. They know that with all their pleas and offerings they'll never have her. They think of nothing else. Dreaming costs nothing, and the grass is always greener in the next man's yard. Wait till she's caught; as soon as one man touches her, the rest won't want her."

"But they don't want to touch her, or by now they would've grabbed her some dark night. The way they've grabbed us. They prefer her the way she is."

"Why do they want to defile her? She doesn't try to tempt them, and she doesn't go after them."

The old woman was thoughtful, her head sunken between her shoulders, hard and black and bulging as an owl's. Finally she spoke.

"It all depends on how hard you work at it. Today is the Day of the Virgin, exactly three years since She came to us. Go make a big celebration, with plenty of wine. We can even have a procession, put the Virgin on an altar at the wharf. Father

· *Open Door*

Antonio never refuses these things. Then choose a man. Point him out to me, and I'll see that he goes after María."

Silently, the women went home and began frying fish cakes and shrimp for the fiesta. Bent over their stoves, they laughed to themselves as they thought about the night, the wine, and the humiliation of María.

In the afternoon they set up tables and benches facing the wharf. They framed the altar with paper flowers and set huge jugs of wine all around. At sunset the boats crossed the sandbar, one behind the other. Farther down the shore, María was playing in the cold waves again, her hair streaming like Medusa's. Not one of them could decide to stop his boat, and they entered the mouth of the harbor in single file. As they sailed in, they heard the sounds of Olimpio's accordion. Drawing closer to port, they could see the tables, the oil lamps, the jugs of wine, and the altar. "It's the Day of Our Virgin, the Day of Our Virgin," the inflamed women shouted from the land.

There was a certain tension at the fiesta. The men were thinking about María, who was swimming in the sea bloodied by the setting sun. But with the wine and the pungent smell of salmon roasting on the hot coals, they relaxed. Father Antonio decided the time had come to lead his parishioners to the church.

The Virgin was taken from Her canopy to ride through the village. Dust hardened the lace borders of Her gown, while the fishermen intoned songs that they believed were psalms but which sounded more like the woeful ballads of drunken sailors. The procession ended when She was placed in front of the improvised altar.

They lit candles to Her and stood there gazing at Her, as if waiting for the miracle. The women took advantage of the confusion to serve more wine. They began to dance around the tables and on top of the tables, their petticoats whirling furiously. The sober wharfs had never witnessed anything like it, but who could care about traditions when the honor of the village was at stake? Only old Raquel remained at the altar, as if submerged in prayers. Finally she spoke to the women.

"The time has come. Choose your man and I'll do the rest."

"Not my husband," one woman said.

"Not mine either. Nor my father. Nor my brother. Nor my son."

The old woman was angry. "So you made the fiesta in order to throw it away? You must make a sacrifice to the Virgin, and then you'll live in peace."

But the women were stubborn. Raquel walked away mumbling.

"Call Hernán Cavarrubias, who has no wife or mother or daughter. He deserves María," a woman shouted after her. For a brief moment old Raquel was silent. Finally she went looking for Cavarrubias. She told him that she had had a vision: María loved him and was calling him, she was hiding somewhere in the village because her desire made her shy. He must take her by force because that was what she liked.

"It's a miracle. The Virgin has listened to me because I offered Her my lantern," he said. The wine gave him courage, and he ran off to find María and make her his.

With each glass they served, the women spread the news. There was not a man on the wharf who didn't know about Hernán Cavarrubias and who was not consumed by envy. Cavarrubias returned much sooner than expected, defeated.

"María's gone. She isn't at home or on the streets or at the store or on the beach. The earth has swallowed her up."

The men thought that perhaps the sea had swallowed her; it was better that way, because now they could continue to desire her as before. Meanwhile, Cavarrubias was bitterly lamenting his fate, trying to extract some consolation from the Virgin. Suddenly he realized that it was all Her fault.

"The Virgin is to blame," he shouted. "In spite of the lan-

· *Open Door*

tern, She made me look bad. She never loved us. We have never gotten anything from Her, have we?"

At the other end of the wharf, the women were whispering, reproaching themselves for having sent the one-armed man instead of one of their own to end the myth of María. Finally one of them lifted her head above the group and spoke out.

"It's not our fault. We asked the Virgin for help and this is what She does. We were only after what was ours, our men wanting us. Nothing that could have offended Her. If She didn't do us the favor, it's because She wanted to humiliate us."

Little by little, a crowd had gathered in front of the Virgin, with the full measure of accumulated grudges and prayers. Someone lowered Her from the altar, and the reproaches were hurled at Her with fury. A judgment was quickly reached, and the penalty executed. Hernán Cavarrubias hurled the first stone.

tr. Hortense Carpentier and J. Jorge Castello

The Son

of

Kermaria

The children's laughter echoed from the main road, and three old women dressed in black made the sign of the cross. It was the bitter laughter of tired men, of demons, and the old women, who no longer trembled before anything, did tremble when they heard that shrill, discordant laughter.

"I'm the doctor. . . ."

"I'm Death. . . ."

"I'm a rich man. . . ."

"I'm Death. . . ."

"I'm Death. . . ."

"Dummy! You can't have two Deaths, one after the other. You have to be a pauper, or the butcher, or anything, but you know you can't be Death, not if it isn't your turn."

"I can if I want to," Joseph said. "After all, I'm the one who invented this game, I'm the one who showed all of you the painting in the chapel, I'm . . ."

Needless to say, they didn't let him finish. They had a very

· *Open Door*

personal idea of justice, and they were quick to act with their fists. Shouting, "No favorites," they jumped on poor Joseph. He ran away as fast as his eleven-year-old legs would carry him. As if he hadn't been the one who proposed the game of imitating the circle of living and dead that was painted in the Kermaria chapel. On those oppressive summer days when everyone else slept all afternoon, Joseph's grandfather took him to see the seven-hundred-year-old painting. In the silence of the gray chapel, the boy would describe the flaking contours of the macabre dance to the blind old man.

"There's a skeleton," he would tell him, "taking the hand of a man in a long cape and a flat black hat. The man is a lawyer, and he goes hand in hand with Death. Everyone has his own private Death, no one can escape Her, and She makes you dance and dance and won't let you go for anything."

The grandfather would get enthusiastic at this point. "Go on, keep telling me," he'd say, and he would break into a dance on the worn tile floor, bumping against the straw chairs and the prayer desks. The old man certainly knew how to imitate the figures in the fresco and dance like them; for he was closer to death than anyone was, and he must have felt that bony hand firmly clutching his own.

Joseph admired his grandfather, even if he did spend the entire day swaying back and forth in his rocking chair in the middle of the patio, facing the chicken coop, humming unintelligible songs to himself. And because he admired him, Joseph went to him whenever he needed consolation after a humiliating skirmish with the other children. Often, the old man, deep in his daydreams, wouldn't hear him arrive.

"They must be washing Her. I hear the splashing of water on Her flanks; She must be fresh, taut, and rosy. I'd like to undress myself and roll around on the cold stone slabs and wash these damned eyes of mine, which must be renewed and blessed, with the water that has run off Her body."

"Grandfather!" Joseph grabbed him by the arm and shook him. "Grandfather!"

The rocking chair stopped.

"Joseph, is it you? Go see if they're washing Her, I want to know. Now I hear the brush running over Her rosy flesh. . . ."

"Yes, they're washing Her, all right. Last night Constantine the hunchback climbed in through a window and slept under the altar tapestry. Son of a bitch! He must have left the poor thing full of fleas."

"Constantine the hunchback, Constantine the hunchback, and they don't let me get near Her because those damned old women scream to high heaven when they see me. They don't even let me touch Her. All because I once buried my face in the basin of holy water and cooled my lips on the lips of the Virgin. In the chapel of Kermaria, of all places, as if She weren't at home there, and I with Her, in the house that belongs to everyone."

"Those old women are witches," Joseph said to comfort him, caressing the little bag of rock salt that hung from his neck to protect him from evil. Then the old man laughed as he remembered the time the children took the polychromed apostles, gigantic Romanesque wood carvings, out of the niches in the Kermaria atrium, then installed themselves in the niches—twelve children with dirty faces, dressed in rags, standing absolutely still and waiting eagerly to frighten the old women who would come at dawn to first Mass.

"Of course they're witches," the grandfather echoed. "I know that better than anybody; I could see it when I was a boy. Always the same, skinny and black. They never change, they never die. They cast the spells that made me blind because I was the only man who went to the chapel and saw them kneeling there, jumbling up their prayers in front of the Virgin and the Child, the Child who didn't know what to do with that big round breast the Virgin offered Him. There they were, pray-

· Open Door

ing for the milk in the breasts of every mother to turn sour, so that at night all the children would turn into owls or wolves." The old man fell silent.

"They're witches," Joseph insisted, to get him to go on talking. He didn't want to hear the silence, because at that moment he caught sight of his mother sneaking out through the back gate, and he was afraid to hear her steps going off toward a fate that could only be terrible and mysterious. She wasn't like other women, though; she was still young and beautiful and she had only begun to wear black when her husband died, a few years ago.

"All of them are witches, that's right, and they made me blind. But what they don't know is that I can now lick the rough walls of Kermaria and feel those walls inside me more than ever, even if the stone tears my skin."

Seated on the pressed-earth floor of the patio, Joseph dug his nails into the palm of his hand and wondered where his mother had gone. But nothing could hold him like the old man's words, and he chose to stay rather than run off to find out the truth; to stay and store up warm memories for the cold nights at boarding school, when his imagination would take him back to Kermaria chapel and he would lick its rough, ridged walls or roll on the floor or purify himself by drinking all the holy water. And yet, when vacation time came, his tongue would be cut by the granite, the floor would feel too hard, the holy water taste too stale. He was lucky Father Medard didn't shoo him out with a broom.

"In a few days the pilgrimage will begin," the grandfather said, interrupting Joseph's thoughts.

The pilgrimage was the most important event of the year for the parish of Kermaria in Ifkuit, forgotten in the middle of the Breton underbrush, far from the sea, from the mountain air, simply clinging to the earth with its poor isolated mud houses with blackened thatched roofs. But the group of wild children who hung around the chapel didn't share the pilgrims' joy; they felt dispossessed by the people who came from the most distant corners of Brittany to ask for the good health and physical strength that none of the cathedrals with delicate steeples could offer. So, well ahead of time, the children made elaborate preparations to make their presence felt and to uphold the honor of the village with troublemaking while their mothers stayed away from the chapel.

The women who came were fishermen's wives, from the coast, and they brought with them the memory of an ancient myth, the antiquity of a race, and the smell of the sea. The women of Kermaria inhaled deeply to fill their lungs with the salty odor.

The children, however, were insensitive to the smell of salt air. All they wanted was to get close to Father Medard during Mass so they could make themselves dizzy with the smell of the incense that was lavished only during the pilgrimage.

Joseph was the only one who knew something about the sea and the mystery of its foam. During the past summer, his mother, more silent than ever, had taught him to weave as they sat around the family table after supper. At the head of the table, the old man hummed and enjoyed his glass of brandy. He usually chided a bit before being taken to bed.

"Weave, my children. Make socks for my feet that must be warm in winter," he would say, or, "A scarf, I want it long. Don't skimp on the wool—this is going to be a very cold winter, and this poor old man needs warmth."

Mother and son worked silently, not listening to the grandfather's words, not bothering to answer him. Everything was peaceful until one night when the old man reached out and touched the soft wool. His fingers slipped through the open weave, and he thought that all the cold in the world would slip through, too. He didn't realize that his daughter-in-law and grandson were weaving nets.

· *Open Door*

Joseph had fun weaving nets. What's more, he had his mother next to him, and that helped him forget the days when she disappeared at midday and didn't return until dusk.

The preparations for the pilgrimage were also fun. Little by little, the chapel of Kermaria would take on a halo of cleanliness, and the sky set free a soft, steady rain to wash its sides. The children worshiped the grandfather at this time, because they felt they were losing the chapel and they thought he was the only person who could bring it back. Covered with mud, they would sit on the wet floor on rainy afternoons and listen to him talk, as if he were a prophet of Kermaria, which for them was alive and had a soul.

Father Medard would pace back and forth in front of the shed and never miss an opportunity to scold the children. "Children, go back to your homes. Our Father's eyes are upon you, and He knows what you are up to." He knew what to expect when the parish children got together with the old man, and he was uneasy. But the children only laughed their bitter laughter and spoke in low voices.

At last the day of the pilgrimage arrived. Minutes before evening Mass, the blacksmith's son brought a jar filled with live spiny-finned fish and dumped them into the basin of holy water. The other children filed into the chapel with sullen expressions and sat in the back pews scowling, waiting for the first pilgrims.

Joseph's mother came in with a group of strangers. She dipped her fingers into the holy water cautiously, for she had seen the fish, and her face showed no surprise. With the sad look that had settled in her eyes over the last few years, she caught a fish between her hands and left the chapel, tiptoeing, trying not to be noticed. But Joseph saw her and decided to slip away after her, even if it meant missing the sight of the old women absentmindedly dipping their fingers into the basin of small slippery shapes.

He was going to run after her, but at the threshold a sudden flash of sunlight hurt his eyes, which had become accustomed to the semidarkness of the chapel and the persistent gray drizzle, and he had to stop. When he opened his eyes again, he saw a white form disappearing behind the thorny bushes at the side of the main road, across from the chapel.

Joseph spent an hour within the tangled woodland looking for his mother. The undergrowth stretched toward him like fingers, scratching his legs and tearing his clothes. Each tree, each bush, each crippling plant had its own thorns, long or short, black, white, or orange; he saw them in detail or not at all, so distraught was he in his desperate search. "I have to find her," he told himself. And then, "I hope I never find her." He didn't want his fears confirmed. He didn't know exactly why he was afraid, for he had crossed the circle of demons surrounding the chapel a thousand times. But now something more vital was at stake, something that was part of his flesh and blood. If his mother had wanted to find herself a new husband (at least he was sure of that much), she had betrayed him miserably by not choosing one of the apostles in the church patio or one of the figures in the fresco who were his real friends.

His mother had once told him that to love one has to be mature, wise, and full of piety. He had answered, "When I fall in love, my children will have the face of the wax Child in front of the altar."

The blood from his scratches was streaming down his face, his arms, his legs, and he felt all the heat of the nettles. He finally spotted her at the bottom of the ravine. His eye had been caught by the unusual sight of her splendid white dress. Cautiously he moved a bit closer. In the palm of her hand was the fish, no longer alive.

He sat at the top of a hill behind a thicket and waited. He knew something was going to happen, for his mother had never done anything like this before. Far away, the bell of Kermaria broke the silence, marking the end of evening Mass.

· *Open Door*

The wait was long, and Joseph grew agitated. Perhaps his mother had not betrayed him, perhaps the man she was waiting for really belonged to the chapel and was none other than Father Medard. But then, on an open path between the thorny bushes, a man appeared—very tall, blond, strong-limbed. Joseph recognized him by his walk as the fisherman who journeyed inland every Friday to sell fish to the parish of Kermaria.

Joseph could only see his mother's back, but by the way her shoulders quivered, he guessed what the look in her eyes must be—so much her own, deep and sad, fixed on the man approaching her.

The fisherman walked over to the woman and took her by the shoulders with his big open hands, and she began to rise, slowly. Joseph didn't want to witness the meeting of those eager lips, and he cried out, "Mama!"

And then he wanted to roll over and over on the thorns and to be beaten very hard, so the pain he felt inside would go out of him and mingle with the healthy, familiar pain of the flesh. But the blows didn't come, and when he finally opened his eyes, his mother was standing alone in front of him, her hands limp at her sides.

They walked back to the farm in silence, and there, mother and son stayed shut in for several days. She spoke only to ask, "What do you know about the sea?" and sometimes she shook him until he cried. Joseph licked his tears, thinking they were the only salt water in the world.

In the meantime, the grandfather wandered about the main road in the rain. When he heard footsteps, he would approach the passersby and ask for something to eat because he had been forsaken. The neighbors felt sorry for him, but they couldn't forget his affronts to Kermaria, and they shouted obscenities and insults at him.

"Why don't you go to the chapel and swallow wafers and eat candles and get indigestion! Idiot!"

"Time and again you drank the wine that was meant for

Mass. Why not do it again instead of begging for the wine from our tables?"

But, like a litany, the grandfather kept on begging: "Pity for a poor blind man . . ."

"It isn't pity you need, but a swat on the behind."

Nevertheless, they let him sleep in the fresh hay in their barns, and they painted his walking stick white, and he was a guest at many tables while his daughter-in-law kept herself shut in.

"What do you know about the sea?" she would scream at Joseph at night. And Joseph, his eyes open wide, tried to see her in the dark as he chewed on a bit of stale bread that he had been hiding in his pocket.

Finally, one morning, the sun came out again, the same sun that had shone the afternoon of the pilgrimage and then disappeared behind the gray cloak of the drizzle. His mother packed the sausages that were left in the pantry and made Joseph get dressed quickly and go out.

They arrived at Ploumanac'h at sunset, not because it was a long way off but because they had had a hard time finding someone who would take them there.

"Is this the harbor? It can't be, it can't be," Joseph's mother exclaimed, biting the palm of her hand and looking despairingly at the dry harbor, forsaken by the tide, where the big-bellied fishing boats lay on the rosy sand.

It can't be, but it is, Joseph thought happily. His lips were about to stretch into a timid smile of triumph, when in the distance he saw a man approaching, and he recognized his mother's fisherman. The fisherman had recognized them, too, and was walking right toward them. Without warning, Joseph freed himself from the hand that was holding him and began to run.

"Joseph, Joseph, come back, don't go away," his mother

· *Open Door*

cried, and then, "Ah, Pierre, make my boy come back. Don't let him run away from me."

They began to chase after Joseph. His mother couldn't stop crying. "I wanted to find you again, Pierre, but not to lose him. I came to look for you, I swear it. Catch him, for God's sake, catch him. . . ."

Joseph's hair fell over his eyes. He wanted to escape from that man, yet he didn't want to be parted from his mother. But she was on the man's side, so there was nothing he could do but run with all his might. At moments he felt their voices almost on top of him and he was frightened; but he was even more frightened when the sound of their calling grew distant, and he thought he would never find his way back again.

At last he saw a big door that led to a church courtyard, and he walked in. He knew he was on friendly ground when he had the churchyard stones under his feet, and he stopped to inhale deeply and release a long sigh that echoed in the bell tower. It was beginning to grow dark, and the last violet lights were disappearing behind the stone crucifix and the vault with its fine columns. That would be the best refuge, he thought, nobody would think of looking for him there. Since he was small, he could slip through the narrow opening between columns and sit on the enormous pile of human bones, gray and crumbling, disinterred over a long period of time to make room in the small cemetery for new bones, dead flesh, worms.

All the terror that was floating around finally overcame him, and he shivered. He would have howled like a dog had he not been afraid he might sound like a soul in pain.

To protect himself against ghosts and evil lights, he shut his eyes tight, and he covered his ears with his arms to shut out the moans of the dead. But every so often he cheated and slackened his arms so he could hear if they were still calling his name in the distance, or he peeked through his half-closed eyes to search for some human silhouette.

When the moon came out, he saw the empty eye sockets of skulls fixed on him and, beyond the columns, the crucifix and the bleak profile of the church.

By then fear had become so much a part of his flesh, it almost didn't bother him. He was exhausted by the long trip, the flight, and the fear. He thought that perhaps it wasn't so bad that his mother was going away with a man who was very much alive and who didn't belong to the damned world of the dead. As his head fell on a pile of bones, he thought that the affection he needed and could no longer have from his mother might come from that other woman in his village, so large, so warm, so generous: the chapel of Kermaria.

tr. Hortense Carpentier and J. Jorge Castello

· *Open Door*

The Minstrels

"Why do you keep asking what they are called? You already know. I've told you twenty times, letter by letter, syllable by syllable. Why do you ask me again?"

The boy didn't realize that he was torturing her, and he lowered his head, hurt, biting his lips. The pitch-black hair fell over his forehead. He didn't want to anger her; their name was not what mattered. What did matter was the word from his mother's lips. When she said it, a small bell-like sound broke loose in her voice, the voice that was sometimes sad but at other times resonated with deep pleasure. Of course, he wasn't going to insist, that wasn't a man's way. Rather it was to pretend indifference. He reached over to pick up a pebble that lay on the ground between the hind legs of the cow, a perfect pebble, the kind that shatters when it is thrown against the hard barn wall. As the boy bent over, the docile cow's tail swatted him in the face, and his mother laughed.

"They were called the Minstrels." The name burst out of her.

The boy raised his head as soon as she spoke, but it was too late. He could only catch the last notes of her laugh, in which there was neither the pain nor the anguish that he liked to hear behind the gaiety.

There was no one like his mother in the entire village of Le Bignon. People respected her even though she always asked for credit and even though her name was Jeanne, a peasant's name. He was called Ariel. Ariel loved and hated his name. He repeated it at night when he was alone in his high bed, buried in the thick woolen mattress that swallowed up sounds, or when he walked through the fields during threshing time and saw the men at work in the distance, or when he romped in the fresh sweet-smelling hay. Ariel . . . But when he had to say it in school, when the bigger children taunted him and asked, "What's your name, pretty boy?" and patted his head, expecting his hair to be soft and silky rather than hard and wild as in fact it was, all he could do was turn around and run. From afar he would shout, "Ariel, Ariel," regretting his cowardice.

On those afternoons of flight, he would return to the farm burning with shame. The three miles on foot from the small town of Meslay to Les Maladières were not enough to cool his cheeks. He left the asphalt road reluctantly, and he took no pleasure in slipping down into the muddy path or kicking the fragile pebbles or leaning against the withered apple tree. On those days of shame (shame at not having had the courage to say his name) he didn't greet the neighbors or bend over the duck pond to find the goldfish that lived at the bottom of the grayish-green water. And, finally, when he pushed open the rickety wooden gate at Les Maladières, he did not run to the small barn where his mother usually was milking the cow at that hour of dusk.

On those days she would call him.

· *Open Door*

"Ariel!"

That call had a dry and special sound; he felt relieved and ran to take refuge in her warm skirt, between her open legs and under the cow's udder. She would hand him his bowl of warm milk, and Ariel was purified as he listened to her sweet voice.

"You have Yves's eyes, blue and deep. Yves was the one who loudly sang happy songs. He shouted them, almost, and I trembled with fear: the Germans might hear him and take all of them away from me. You have the same eyes as Yves. . . . I looked at them a great deal and I wanted to keep him with me."

Mother and son sat silent, surrounded by the warm smell of the barn, buried in their thoughts of Yves, while the cow lowed with impatience.

On other occasions, Jeanne the Strong One (as they called her in the village where she grew up) would tell her son, "You have Antoine's hands . . . long and slender, not pudgy like mine, and he played the mandolin like an angel playing the harp."

Or else, "Your hair is as bristly as those thickets out there, just like Joseph's. . . ."

And Ariel would leap up and shake her arm until it hurt. "No, Mama, no! You told me it was Alexis's hair. Have you forgotten already?"

And Jeanne the Strong One would laugh with that delicate and sad laugh he loved so much.

"How could I forget? You're right; Joseph's hair was black too, but soft to the touch. But Alexis's was hard, like yours. I used to laugh because he couldn't comb it. I'll never forget that."

It had all begun on a very clear May morning. Georges Le Gouarnec, her husband, had just gone off to the war. "I see they need drunkards now," Jeanne had said to him in farewell. He walked away and then came back, not to kiss his wife but to put the last two bottles of homemade brandy in his knapsack.

He had left her alone on the farm. She did what she could, but the old tractor stayed idle in the shed, she had to hire men to sow and harvest her small farm, and most of the apples rotted on the ground because she couldn't make cider, nor did it interest her. When spring came, and the farm work made too many demands on her, she began to miss her Georges.

Nevertheless, on those May mornings she felt lighthearted and almost ran as she drove the flock of geese to the feeding trough. She would have liked to toss her long-handled pick into the air and dance with her skirts swinging above her rubber boots. The geese cackled as usual, with their beaks pointing to the sky, seemingly in ill humor. She screamed at the geese until she saw them coming, singing softly as they walked down the dirt road that went past the duck farm and the neighboring farmhouses. She could barely hear their song, but Jeanne knew that something sweet was being sung by the way they swayed together, like the poplars in front of the church in the breeze of autumn dusks.

She closed her eyes and counted them as if they were engraved in her memory: there were nine. Impossible. You can't have nine identical human beings. Maybe two, or three at the most; her loneliness had played a nasty trick on her and multiplied the men. She opened her eyes and saw them clearly against the rough wall of the farmhouse. They had stopped singing and stood in a row facing the geese. There were nine, truly, each one different although each back was curved in the same way under the weight of a knapsack.

Jeanne wanted to go closer to them; she felt the heat of the goose feathers against her legs and the heat of the men's stares on her face. It had cost her dearly to walk among the flock of geese, and she didn't dare to look directly into the faces of the strangers as she dried her hands on the kitchen towel that hung from her waist.

· *Open Door*

At that moment Ariel raised his head. "Is it something new you're remembering, Mama?"

She set aside her memories to return to her son.

"No, not something new. I've told you everything. There's nothing more for me to remember, only to begin again."

"You were thinking about the day they came. . . ."

"That's true."

"And where was I?"

"Still in heaven. You came down many months later."

"That's why I didn't see them. But are you sure you've told me everything?"

"Very sure."

Not everything. There are things a child of eight cannot be told, even if he has Alexis's hair and Antoine's hands and a voice that promises to be Michel's voice.

Michel was the first, and she had chosen him because he sang better than the rest; he was the soloist, with the deep voice, and when he opened his mouth, everyone else fell silent. Ariel, the voice of Michel. Someday you will have Michel's voice, my son.

They were fleeing from the war, and they had not come upon a better place to hide than this isolated farm in the middle of the poor and wild land of Brittany. Only one barrel of cider was left in the cellar, and Jeanne the Strong One wanted to cry because Georges Le Gouarnec had gone away without preparing more. On the other hand, when he was there and the whole house was filled with the smell of apples, there was that other smell that came from the loft where he kept the still, that other smell that she hated but which she longed to smell again. Brandy, hundreds of bottles, all those Georges Le Gouarnec had drunk throughout his life from morning to night, and which Jeanne would have liked to recover now in order to keep with her the nine men who sang songs and told sad stories.

To keep them. The first night was for Michel, she had decided, and for the first time since her husband's departure she returned to the bedroom and to the high, deep bed where she sank in Michel's company. The others installed themselves in two cots and on the dining room floor.

"What were they called, Mama?"

This time she was caught off guard, and she answered simply, "The Minstrels."

She had already taken the two pails of milk into the house and she was feeding the sow that was about to have piglets. She ordered Ariel to collect the eggs from the henhouse. "Don't break any, like Robert, who always came back with the basket dripping."

Robert had turned out to be the worst of all. He never wanted to pluck the geese or check the tractor motor, even though he had been a mechanic at some time in his life. He knew how to tell marvelous stories, though, and he sat at the table with a large bowl of cider cradled in his hands and talked for hours. The others were much more helpful; they helped her kill the hog and make blood sausages and other meats, which later they took with them when they left. Yet it was Robert's laziness that made Jeanne place all her hopes in him. When he took his turn with her, on the fifth night, she carried the washbowl out to the water pump, where she scrubbed herself in the moonlight. In bed, between the soft quilts, she murmured unfamiliar words to him and lavished new caresses on him, invented for him.

When she got up early the following morning, she looked at his eyes to see if he was going to stay, but he turned over and went back to sleep. When night came, Marcel replaced him in the big bed, and the wheel continued turning.

Jeanne always left her bed in the early hours of morning, and as she gently stepped over the sleeping bodies on the dining room floor, she wanted to shout at them to stay. Later, she

· *Open Door*

would prepare breakfast; the good smell of onion soup woke them, and she no longer worried whether or not they would leave her, for their voices, their smiles, their jokes were filling her life. And when she served them the soup as they sat at the table on the long, narrow benches, she counted them again to be sure of the figure of her happiness. It was nine.

Now it is one, a young one, huddled next to the fireplace on winter nights. Jeanne would have liked to share her warmth with him, but she, too, feels cold, cold inside. She says to him, "Ariel, sing me a song. . . ."

And Ariel, obedient, sings a song he has learned in school:

Sur le pont d'Avignon
L'on y passe, l'on y danse. . . .

"No, Ariel, not that one; a serious song."

With the best intentions, Ariel changes the rhythm and intones *The Marseillaise*.

At other times, Jeanne the Strong One, dispirited, doesn't want songs. "Ariel, my son, tell me a story," she will say.

Ariel will then tell stories he has learned at school, about bad boys and good boys who come to blows, or stories about dogs and cats and horses. These are the only stories he knows. Sometimes he feels encouraged to talk about the goldfish that live at the bottom of the duck pond with the grayish-green water, the shiny fish that only let themselves be seen by people with good hearts. But he prefers not to think about them too much, since he has never actually seen them himself.

One day each year his mother sits him on her knee and tells him the stories she likes to hear. On that day there is no work except for feeding the animals. Ariel doesn't go to school. It is February twenty-first, his birthday. Jeanne the Strong One sits in her low chair, peeling potatoes, tirelessly recounting the stories that the Minstrels had once told her, cheerful stories of princes and shepherdesses. Sometimes the stories are about orgies with women and wine. She can tell these stories to Ariel in spite of his age because they are so ancient that Ariel will not understand them.

What she cannot tell about are the true nights with the Minstrels, nights changed into words that burn her mouth, words that she would like to spit out. But she must keep them to herself: Ariel is her son, only nine years old today, and a son cannot be told these things.

"Mama, how are children born? Like calves? Do they have a father, like the bull we hired last spring?"

"For children it takes nine months, and they all have a father. No one can be born without a father."

Ariel knew that already, but he wanted to be sure: nine months and nine fathers. When he went to bed, he didn't think about Jeanne's stories. He thought that he was the richest little boy in the world, because in order to have him, his mother had hired nine fathers. Alexis's hair; Antoine's hands; Michel's voice; Yves's eyes; Henri's . . .

Lying on the cot in the dining room, Jeanne the Strong One was also thinking about Henri. He was the leader, and he was the first one to talk to her when they arrived at Les Maladières.

"We are the Minstrels," he had said by way of introduction. "The government has given us rifles, but we only want to wield our mandolins. We prefer the ring of our own voices to the sound of bullets. If you, dear madame, would be good enough to give us shelter for a few days, we will try not to compromise you. We will head south as soon as the danger has passed."

They stayed nine days and nine nights, and then they left for the south, singing.

"Ariel! You never pay attention. Repeat what I said. Show me where south is." In the middle of the geography class, and without apparent reason, Ariel would begin to cry.

Jeanne no longer cried. Perhaps she had never cried. She

did all she could to keep them, but they had gone. The one who returned, shortly after, was Georges Le Gouarnec, her legitimate husband.

It seems he came back merely to get a double ration of brandy and to insult her because the whole village knew about her secret guests, even though no one had ever seen them. Nine pairs of horns didn't weigh heavily on his alcohol-filled head, but what the inhabitants of Bignon might say, the chance that they might mock him, that he couldn't endure. He mumbled filthy words and spat on his wife's bare feet as she walked in front of him carrying the tub of dirty clothes to the water pump. But Le Gouarnec's hatred brought to life her memories of the other men, and she stood in front of the pump without pumping, her arms at her sides and her eyes full of dreams.

Georges Le Gouarnec allowed the four seasons of the year to pass, one by one, without tending the wheat that was rotting in the fields. He was only biding his time until the apple juice fermented and he could lock himself up in the loft and tangle himself in the pipes of the still. Exactly one year after his return he left again, a little before Ariel's birth. By this time Jeanne no longer needed the stimulus of his hatred to evoke the men who had brought joy into her life.

"Mama, which one of them loved dogs?"

Jeanne shook her head. Right now she didn't want to think anymore, she didn't want to answer. She would have preferred going to sleep, but she had promised Ariel that she would make plum jam. He watched her, uneasy.

"You've forgotten already, see? I told you that one day you'd forget them and we'd be left without anything. Without them we won't be able to go on living."

Jeanne made a face, but she answered him. "Me, forget? No, it's just that I'm tired."

"Tired of them?"

"Of them, no, my love. Come, let's look at the table where they carved their names."

She passed her hand gently over the table where the names were. Ariel imitated the caress.

The years passed, until one morning Jeanne awoke knowing it was an important day. Ariel was thirteen. Finally she could pour out her heart to him, tell him of her great love for the Minstrels and satisfy the old thirst she had to share the story with someone.

When she walked into the kitchen to light the fire, she found she had to lock her heart away once more: Georges Le Gouarnec had returned after thirteen years of absence, more puffy and red-faced than ever, and he stood facing the oven. When Ariel ran into the kitchen to kiss her, she could only murmur: "Ariel, say hello to your father. . . ." She felt her cheeks burn with shame, sure that Ariel had closed his eyes because he didn't want to see the man.

Georges Le Gouarnec shook him by the shoulders.

"Say hello to your father, stupid!"

Ariel slipped away from the large hand that was clutching him and fled to the fields, burying himself among the thickets.

"I know it isn't him. I know it isn't. The Nine Minstrels are my father, not a fat mean man who smells bad."

Ariel threw himself to the ground, face down, next to the hare's nest he had discovered the day before, and he shut his ears against the old man's shouts. When the stars began to pale in the sky, long after Le Gouarnec had fallen asleep on the thick mattress under the feather quilt, Jeanne the Strong One went to look for her son.

"Mama, Mama, it isn't him, is it?"

"No."

"And you'll never forget them, will you?"

· *Open Door*

"Never, never."

"Mama," he cried, and his voice rose hoarsely.

She realized that the time had come for Ariel to be like them, to follow his own path now that her bed, the one she had shared with them, was creaking under another weight, ordinary, unpleasant.

At sunrise on the following day, on his way to the distant farm where he had been hired to do the milking, Ariel threw nine stones into the duck pond, giving each one a name.

While her husband's redundant snoring rocked the house, Jeanne the Strong One leaned over the names on the table and decided to trace the letters and write Ariel the stories the Minstrels had told.

Ariel wrote her, in turn, that the owner's daughter had gone to Mass in her white dress and that later the dress changed into a pair of wings, taking the owner's daughter to the kingdom of the wild ducks.

Ariel was now telling stories of his own, but Jeanne the Strong One never let him forget the Minstrels; she mentioned them in each of her letters. He didn't realize that the fields grew green, dried and froze, over and over again. He didn't realize that time passed, that three years is almost a lifetime for a boy who had turned thirteen when he left home.

He didn't realize it until that other, hostile letter arrived in a brown envelope reeking of incense. It was from the priest of Bignon. On the envelope it said Ariel Le Gouarnec, not simply Ariel, and he knew it was bad news.

Jeanne the Strong One was dying. Ariel couldn't do anything to stop it, only try to make her say the word that would help her recover part of her strength.

She lay in bed, her hand suddenly fragile, lost in the feather quilt. Ariel squeezed the hand he had known when it was hard and alive.

"Mama, tell me what they were called. . . ."

From the dining room came Le Gouarnec's voice, cracking the silence like a whip. "I never get a greeting or a look from you. Me, your own father. You're a son of a bitch, that's for sure, but I am your father, after all, your poor old father . . ." And the syllables ran together like the brandy spilling over the names on the table.

In the bedroom Ariel tried to control himself, but he shook her hand more furiously each time; he shook her arms, her shoulders.

"Mama, tell me about them. What are they called?"

For an instant he saw a flash of pain in her eyes. He wanted to leave her in peace, he didn't want to shake her hand anymore, to demand anything from her. From the dining room came the grunts, the shouts, the laughter; above all, the laughter.

"He thinks he's the son of God! He thinks he's the son of gods and tumblers, but I spit on all of them and their progeny, because it was this stinking jackass, I, who made you, for glory, peace, and tranquility in my bitter old age. Amen."

Ariel pressed the other hand, unable to control himself any longer.

"Tell me their names. Don't leave me without them."

Jeanne the Strong One turned her face toward the wall, but she forced herself to speak in a thread of a voice.

"I don't remember anymore . . . but go, go find them . . ." and her eyes closed on that small dream.

The curses that Georges Le Gouarnec never stopped mumbling during the three days of the wake were the funeral prayer for Jeanne the Strong One, but so were Ariel's hopes when he left, running toward the south, toward the sun, to find the Minstrels.

tr. Hortense Carpentier and J. Jorge Castello

· *Open Door*

Design by David Bullen
Typeset in Mergenthaler Imprint
with Galliard display
by Wilsted & Taylor
Printed by Haddon Craftsmen
on acid-free paper